"What time will your curfew be?"

She heard his frustration. "It's not like that."

"Then tell me what it is. Here I am, sneaking you home in the middle of the night. Are you going to climb through your bedroom window? Take off your shoes so you can creep inside? Is your dad going to be standing there with a shotgun pointed at me?"

"Tucker, it's not like that."

"Isn't it? Isn't it because of what happened ten years ago?"

Okay, maybe that was part of it. Tucker had already broken up with one Cherry sister. Would it end up being two? She didn't want to put her family through another mess. She didn't want them thinking it was Tucker's fault.

"I want to ease them into it...and I need time."

"Then we'll ease into this..." He sighed deeply and she felt his hunger. "But for now, get out of this truck before I make a grab for you and never let you go."

THE ONE WHO CHANGED EVERYTHING

BY
LILIAN DARCY

First published in Great Britain 2013
by Mills & Boon, an imprint of Harlequin (UK) Limited,
Eton House, 18-24 Paradise Road, Richmond, Surrey TW9 1SR

© Lilian Darcy 2013

ISBN: 978 0 263 90143 6
ebook ISBN: 978 1 472 00531 1

23-0913

Harlequin (UK) policy is to use papers that are natural, renewable and recyclable products and made from wood grown in sustainable forests. The logging and manufacturing processes conform to the legal environmental regulations of the country of origin.

Printed and bound in Spain
by Blackprint CPI, Barcelona

Lilian Darcy has written nearly eighty books for Mills & Boon. Happily married with four active children and a very patient cat, she enjoys keeping busy and could probably fill several more lifetimes with the things she likes to do—including cooking, gardening, quilting, drawing and traveling. She currently lives in Australia but travels to the United States as often as possible to visit family. Lilian loves to hear from readers. You can write to her at PO Box 532, Jamison PO, Macquarie ACT 2614, Australia, or email her at lilian@liliandarcy.com.

Chapter One

Mary Jane was laughing. You could hear it thirty yards away, through a closed door and a screen of bushes, and it was a glorious sound on a mild mid-October Monday beside a mountain lake.

Daisy Cherry came up the steps and out of the delicious fresh air into the resort office and found her sister with shaking shoulders and tears running down her cheeks, a heap of old photo albums in a litter around her, along with piles of shipping boxes, too. "Hey, what's so funny?"

Mary Jane rocked back on her heels, flattened a hand over her heart and gasped for breath. "Dad's mustache, Mom's wedding hat. Their clothes. Her *swimsuit*. I'm sorry, it's not that funny. I don't know why I'm—"

"No, it's great," Daisy cut in with conviction.

As the eldest of the three Cherry sisters at age thirty-four, Mary Jane was too serious and too responsible too much of the time. Right now, her medium brown hair stuck out in a messy halo all over her head, she had dust marks on her cream-colored top and she looked like someone who'd been working harder than she should, for longer than she could remember.

Daisy and Mary Jane had already had a few tense moments with each other since Daisy had come back east to live just a couple of weeks ago, and in all honesty, Daisy didn't think that she was to blame. It was really good to see Mary Jane lose control, lighten up a little, and Daisy found herself grinning at the sight of it.

Unfortunately, the laughter and lost control didn't last.

"I don't have time for this." Mary Jane took a determined hold of herself, stood up, wiped the tears from her eyes with a crumpled tissue and fussed around getting the albums back in a pile, which she dumped into a cardboard box.

"Where did you find them?"

"Here in the office, under a pile of files. Lord only knows what they were doing here."

"Are you packed?" Daisy asked.

"You mean this?" Mary Jane waved her hand at the boxes, some filled, some still empty. "These are going to South Carolina to the new condo with Mom and Dad."

"I meant for your trip, not Mom and Dad's move."

"In that case, I was packed a week ago." Mary Jane looked a little tense suddenly.

She was leaving tomorrow. She loved to travel, and when Spruce Bay Resort closed each year for most of November and April, during the quietest seasons in New York's Adirondack Mountains, she always went away. Someplace exotic, or someplace indulgent. Never the same destination twice. Taking full advantage of the fact that she was single, even though Daisy strongly suspected that in her secret heart Mary Jane didn't actually *want* to be single at all.

This unwanted condition was down to Alex Stewart, horrible man. Water under the bridge, four years on. Nobody talked about it anymore, but Mary Jane had wasted a lot of time—years of her life—on a relationship that had gone nowhere and it had taken its toll on her heart and her outlook.

Mary Jane and I are so different, Daisy had thought to herself more than once. Mary Jane's love for Alex had been a steadfast flame that refused to die even when it needed to. Whereas Daisy had blown hot and cold. Came on strong, then pulled right back. Sent clear signals, then turned them off like a faucet.

I jumped in too fast. I never looked below the surface. It was my fault as much as Michael's.

Was it a fair accusation to make about herself? She still tied herself in knots asking that question. It was a big reason why she was here, instead of in California, and Mary Jane had accused her—quite gently and sympathetically, which almost made it worse—of coming back for the wrong reasons.

"I don't want you as a business partner at Spruce Bay just because you're running away from something that turned sour in your personal life."

This year, because of the renovation and their parents' retirement from the business, Spruce Bay had closed a month early, missing out on the fall-foliage season, and Mary Jane would be spending most of October, including her thirty-fifth birthday on the eighteenth of the month, on safari in the heart of Africa.

She hadn't wanted to go initially. "I'll have to skip my usual trip this year, with the remodel. It just can't be helped." She was definitely too responsible about things like this. Daisy and Mom and Dad—and Lee, from a distance, in Colorado—had all insisted that of course she should go, as usual, since she loved her travels so much. Eventually and reluctantly, Mary Jane had booked her tour package.

"If you're worried I can't handle things here for three weeks, don't be," Daisy assured her quickly now, because her sister had really started to look stressed. "Hey, if I can create the dessert recipes and oversee their preparation every night for a two-hundred-seat five-star San Francisco restaurant, I can oversee a construction crew. I've brainstormed a heap of ideas for the restaurant remodel, I'm so excited about it, and I have menu ideas to match."

"Listen, I don't doubt that, okay?"

"But you doubt the reasons I'm here."

"Sometimes you dive in too fast, Daisy. You told me that happened with Michael. I don't want it happening with Spruce Bay." She gestured toward the open window, where blue sky blazed behind a silhouette of pine needles whose fragrance Daisy could smell from here. She could hear the pine needles, too—the light soughing they made in the breeze. The peace and familiarity of this place hurt her heart, it was so beautiful.

"It won't happen, Mary Jane," she answered, quietly sure of herself, suddenly. "Spruce Bay is different. Spruce Bay is home."

Mary Jane looked at her curiously. "Is that how you feel? Even after ten years away?"

"It is. More than I expected. It hit me just now. I love it here."

"Well, okay, then."

A new peace settled between them.

"And as for the landscaping," Daisy continued after a moment, "it makes much more sense to have the structural work for that done when Spruce Bay is already closed for the interior work, rather than waiting until spring. Obviously the actual planting will have to wait, but that's only a small part of what needs doing."

"True," Mary Jane conceded. "We're behind on the planning for all that. The decisions and plans on the interiors took more time than I expected, especially the cabins, and Mom and Dad have been stalling. They think the grounds are fine as they are."

"They're not."

"I know. But maybe it's too late and we'll have to leave it till spring after all."

"No, we won't, because I called Reid Landscaping yesterday, and I've set up a meeting for tomorrow. I'm hoping that if we can make our decisions and plans quickly, work can get started—"

Mary Jane stood up, looking horrified, and didn't wait to hear when it was that Daisy hoped work would start. "You what?"

"Set up a meeting. Tomorrow at ten."

"With Reid Landscaping." It wasn't a question. More of a thud. Like the dropping of a shoe. All the more obvious because just a few seconds ago they'd had a strong moment of closeness.

"They're the best in the area," Daisy pointed out briskly. "And we've known—"

"*Tucker Reid's* company?"

"Yes."

The simmering stress behind Mary Jane's recent bout of laughter burst through the facade and came out as anger. "You *cannot* be so clueless, Daisy! Tucker Reid!"

"Wait a second..."

"*Tucker. Reid!*" You could have cut the fake patience in Mary Jane's tone with a knife.

Oh, for crying out loud! It wasn't as if Daisy wasn't getting this. Of course she got it!

"It was ten years ago, Mary Jane," she said, gentleness not quite winning out over frustration. Here was her older sister sniping at her again. "It was a broken engagement, not an acrimonious divorce, and it was mutual. Lee and Tucker announced their decision together, remember. Not to mention that Lee is two thousand miles away in Colorado."

Lee, the middle Cherry sister, the meat in the sandwich between responsible, energetically organized Mary Jane and not-nearly-as-blonde-as-she-looked baby sister Daisy.

"Do you honestly not have any idea?" Mary Jane cut in. She was angry. Needlessly angry, Daisy thought. "Do you honestly not know why Lee and Tucker canceled their wedding?"

"I was there, wasn't I? Because they realized it wasn't right, and weren't dumb enough to take such a step when they weren't one hundred percent sure. Because Lee wasn't ready. And Tucker wasn't, either. They were pretty young. I think it was a very wise decision."

"She was twenty-three, he was twenty-four. Not that young. We were all so incredibly happy when they got engaged. Do you honestly think that breaking it was her choice?"

"Lee is incredibly happy with her life now."

"Now. Yes. But it took a while. It took a *long* while. Years." Mary Jane said that last word as if she knew all about things taking years. Alex Stewart again.

"And you're saying that's all because of Tucker Reid?"

"He dumped her! They might have pretended that it was mutual, but it wasn't. It was down to two things." Mary Jane checked the first one off on her fingers. "Because of the accident, and because—" But even though the second finger came up, she stopped abruptly, closed her mouth, and the second reason didn't get spoken.

Daisy's attention had caught on the first reason, however. "The accident? Really? You think it was down to that? Because Lee had some scarring?"

"In large part, yes." But she sounded hesitant and awkward.

"You think Tucker is as superficial as that?" Daisy was shocked about it, for some reason. Disappointed. It had never occurred to her to question the motives of Lee's ex in such a way. She'd taken the whole canceled wedding at face value. They'd both had second thoughts. They'd sensibly called it off. It happened.

She'd been twenty-one years old at the time, and excitedly absorbed in her own life. She remembered giving her first impression of Tucker in a drawled aside to her mother. "Well, he certainly seems like the strong silent type…"

She hadn't meant it as a compliment, but it hadn't been a statement of dislike, either. She'd shared the family's happiness about the upcoming wedding and had thought of Tucker as someone who'd be great for Lee, but not for herself—definitely not her type.

"Do Mom and Dad think this, too?" she asked her sister.

"Mom and Dad think it even more," Mary Jane retorted with spirit. "But that's because they never saw—" She stopped suddenly, and her face was shuttered.

"No one has ever said this!"

"They've said so plenty to me. You haven't been here. And when you are here, usually Lee is here, too, so we don't talk about it."

"Plus it was ten years ago," Daisy reminded her.

"There's that," Mary Jane conceded. She'd calmed

down a little. The angry pink in her cheeks began to fade. The violent eddies of emotion filling the room began to settle. Daisy wondered just how much Alex Stewart had to do with all this, how much Mary Jane was still regretting the fruitless years she'd spent waiting for him to get serious, make the full commitment, and then he never had.

After a moment she said, treading carefully, "Is there something else going on, Mary Jane? You seem—"

Wrong thing to say. "Oh, because it couldn't possibly be *you,* could it? Or Tucker himself, for that matter. It has to be me."

"Well, no, okay, but if there is something, if there's ever anything, I want you to know that you can talk to me, that's all."

She reached out her hand and touched Mary Jane's arm, and at least her sister didn't throw her off. The atmosphere between them eased a little, once more. They were sisters, after all. There was a strong bond, even when they disagreed.

"Look, you're going to Africa," Daisy continued. "It's going to be amazing."

"Y-yes. Oh, it is!"

"I'm sure you still have a ton of stuff to do to get ready. I do understand what you're saying. I'm…a little shocked, actually."

"Shocked?"

"About Tucker."

Mary Jane muttered something that was impossible to hear.

"You said there were two reasons…"

"Yeah, well, no, not really. No."

"You said—"

"Look, that's not important." There was a stubborn set to Mary Jane's mouth now that told Daisy she could spend all day trying to coax more out of her sister and still get next to nothing.

"Let me talk to Lee," she offered, letting the was-there-or-was-there-not-a-second-reason thing go. "And I'll talk to Tucker himself. If there really does seem to be a good reason not to go ahead, our meeting tomorrow is just the initial consult so that he can put together an estimate if we ask him to. We're not committed yet. And if some of his personal choices and attitudes aren't quite what they should be, does that matter? I mean, it's…yeah, disappointing…"

Mary Jane huffed out an impatient breath as if she could have come up with a different word.

"But he'll be doing our landscaping, and that's all," Daisy continued. "It's a business arrangement. It's not like he'll be part of the family, the way we once wanted. It's not as if we need to love everything about him."

"Lee—"

"Lee is way stronger than you think. She's—" *A lot happier about being single than you are, sis.*

Daisy managed not to say it out loud, while Mary Jane retorted, "Lee was way more upset than *you* think about the canceled wedding."

"But since none of this actually *involves* Lee because she has a whole life that she loves, ski instructing and mountain guiding in Colorado, that she's not planning to change anytime soon—"

"Oh, I give up," Mary Jane muttered and stalked into the front office, closing the door very firmly behind her just in case Daisy was in any doubt that the conversation was over.

"You know what?" Daisy said out loud to the empty room. "I give up, too!"

* * *

That statement wasn't quite true, however. She hadn't given up at all. Why else would she have found herself forty minutes later, wearing a fresh outfit, climbing out of her car in the parking lot at the front of Reid Landscaping's building? She'd tried to call Lee to talk about all this, but Lee's phone was switched off, so she'd left a message.

She didn't have an appointment with Tucker. That was tomorrow. But if there was any chance of hosing down Mary Jane's overreaction before she flew off to Africa tomorrow, then why not go after it. You had to put the right energy into a problem if you wanted results. Daisy put energy into everything she did.

The headquarters of Reid Landscaping was an impressive advertisement for the company's abilities. She hadn't seen it before. Ten years earlier, the landscaping business had been only an ambitious plan simmering in Tucker's head that he hadn't spoken of very much, even to Lee. Since then, and having lived in California until so recently, Daisy had never happened down this quiet street on the edge of the woods during vacation visits home.

She'd never bumped into Tucker himself, either, and she knew nothing about his life now. He could be married with two or three children, or seriously attached. He could be divorced, for that matter, or wedded to his career, or maybe a player with no plans ever to settle down.

The building itself was a gorgeous, purpose-built structure in modern log cabin style, with richly varnished golden wood and huge double-glazed, south-facing windows that would catch the sun at all the right times. On the upper level, there seemed to be a private apartment with a balcony orientated to face summer sunsets. A round wooden table and two chairs invited the idea of cool drinks on warm, lazy evenings, while now, in fall, there were wooden tubs planted with chrysanthemums in gold and bronze and deep red.

But it was the exterior landscaping that really showed itself off. Even though the fall foliage had passed its peak of color, everything still looked beautiful. There were plantings that would offer color according to the changes of the season, a long boardwalk-style entrance ramp zig-zagging from the parking lot to the front door, garden features in stone and wood and acid-rusted metal that provided structure to the greenery...

There was much more that Daisy didn't have time to take in right now, but she would definitely want a closer look when it came to planning the detail on the reland-scaping of the Spruce Bay grounds.

She went up the entrance ramp and entered the build-ing, hearing a bell jangling to announce her arrival. "I'm hoping I might be able to see...uh...Mr. Reid for a few minutes. Is he around?" she asked the woman at the main desk. "I'm Daisy Cherry, from Spruce Bay Resort."

"Oh, right, yes, we've spoken. Spruce Bay, that's along the lake between Mission Point and Back Bay? Gorgeous setting. By the way, I'm Jackie. I'm the office manager."

"That's the place. Nice to meet you, Jackie. Some-thing's come up, you see, and I'm hoping for five minutes now, to set us up for the longer meeting."

"Let me check for you."

"Would you? Thanks so much." Daisy sat down in a sleekly comfortable leather chair while Jackie made some finger movements over something on the desktop, appar-ently sending a text message via cell phone to her boss, which meant that Daisy was left not knowing whether Tucker was actually on site or not.

And that was frustrating because she really, really wanted to see him right now, since she really, really didn't want her sister to wing off to Africa in the wrong mood. At times, you could almost suspect that Mary Jane was actively dreading the trip.

Daisy sat, and kept sitting.

Had Tucker checked his phone yet?

Had Lee?

Jackie went on with her work, and Daisy looked around. On the wall to her right there was a whole gallery of photos, beautifully enlarged and mounted. Before-and-after shots of Reid Landscaping projects, candid pictures of the team at work. Here was Tucker himself, perfectly dressed in a dark suit, hair cut short, beard like Orlando Bloom's, accepting an award for a big landscaping project. The award plaque was right here on the wall, also.

And here he was again in another photo, very differently dressed, leaning on a shovel and grinning at the camera. This time he was clean-shaven, his shirtsleeves rolled up, his legs bare and tanned in faded green shorts. He had a couple of staff members standing on either side—a young man with knobby knees and a tall, pretty, fair-skinned brunette with a belt cinching the top of her cargo pants against her very slender waist. It was the closest thing Daisy could find to a personal photo.

Tucker looked the same as he did ten years ago, and yet not. His frame had filled out with more muscle. He had more laugh lines around his eyes, especially when wearing that satisfied, outdoorsy grin.

His presence dominated the whole photo and he looked more confident than he had been the last time they'd met. He gave off a sense of energy and presence, the way a man did when those big plans in his head from years ago have become a reality better than he'd ever dreamed.

And, oh, that grin! Strong and content and full of life. Daisy didn't really recognize the grin, when she thought about it. He'd been tense during those few days she'd spent in his company around the time of the canceled wedding. Prickly and uncomfortable and too watchful sometimes. Strong and silent, as she'd said to Mom. He hadn't grinned much. Had he smiled at all? She hadn't really felt that she'd gotten to know him at all.

With nothing to do but wait, and with Mary Jane's accusations from earlier this morning still fresh in her mind, she found herself thinking back in a way she hadn't done in…oh…*ever.*

Chapter Two

Ten Years Earlier

Lee's fiancé didn't smile.

At all.

"Nice to finally meet you, Daisy," he said, barely moving his lips. Standing beside him and beaming at both of them, Lee didn't seem to notice.

Tucker Reid's face was set like a rock, with a deeply grooved frown between his brows, blue eyes that Daisy couldn't read and a closed, flat mouth. And it wasn't so much that he looked angry or unhappy, he just looked totally determined to keep any expression at all from showing on his face, or let any of the wrong words escape his lips.

She registered the barrier he'd put in place as she shook his hand in greeting, so she let her own smile ebb and just nodded at him and quickly took her hand away from the large, strong grip. "Same back at you. It's about time, isn't it?" Even though the wedding was only five days from now, this was the first time they'd met.

Daisy had been in Paris for a year, and Lee and Tucker had only known each other for a few weeks when she'd flown off to France. They hadn't even been dating at that point and were just friends. They'd both had summer jobs at a big-chain hotel, working long shifts to put some decent money in the bank.

Lee was a rather private person. Even though the rest of the Cherry family was close at hand, they hadn't met Tucker, either, until he and Lee were practically engaged.

Mom, Dad and Mary Jane all adored him, apparently, and were incredibly happy and excited about the wedding.

"He was so wonderful about Lee's accident," Mom had been gushing at regular intervals during the twenty-four hours since Daisy's arrival home, the same way she'd gushed in phone calls and emails while Daisy was in Paris. "He was there by her hospital bed for days on end. She said she couldn't have gotten through the pain without him." Burns hurt a lot, as Daisy knew from her own experience of minor ones in restaurant kitchens. "He never once made her feel it was her fault. He really talked her around on that, because she was beating herself up for being careless with that hot oil in the fryer."

Daisy wasn't sure yet how she was going to feel about Tucker Reid. He stood there while Lee went on talking for just a little too long about how great it was to have all three Cherry sisters together again, and how much had changed over the past year, and how happy she was about absolutely everything.

He gave a tiny nod occasionally, but that was about it, and Daisy decided it was time to extract herself from the whole situation. There was something about the way he was holding himself that wasn't right, something about the look in his narrowed blue eyes, but she didn't have time to think about that. She'd promised to show off her new French dessert-making skills tonight—no, of course she wasn't too tired!—and there was a lot to do in the kitchen.

"Mom, I need to get started on the peach tart and the raspberry dacquoise," she said. "Or I'll crash from jet lag before I'm done."

She undraped the gorgeously patterned and very Parisian fringed silk scarf from around her neck and shoulders and tossed out her hair, itching to get to work.

Mmm, it felt so good to be home, and yet to know herself a little changed from the person she had been the last time she was here. She'd learned so much about fashion and taste and grace and creativity in Paris. She'd spent hours browsing boutiques and galleries and food markets, people watching at pavement cafés, window-shopping, dreaming.

Even though dessert-making was her main creative outlet and her planned profession, she loved to draw, as well, and she'd filled a stack of sketch pads with rapid-fire impressions of Paris and its people. She hadn't wasted a second of the trip.

She felt as if she was bursting with life, bursting with the love of it, its beauty and variety and vibrancy. Lee had the reputation in the Cherry family of being the most energetic of the three girls, but Daisy had decided this wasn't true.

Lee might be incredibly athletic and outdoorsy, just as her fiancé was, but there were other kinds of energy. The energy of her own creativity sizzled inside Daisy, and right now she couldn't wait to get started on those luscious desserts.

On her way to the kitchen, she glanced back at the

bridal couple, still a little thrown by her first meeting with her future brother-in-law—by how little he'd given her, by the fact that she had so little to go on in finding out who he was. Lee was looking up at him and she wasn't smiling and animated anymore. Tucker stood awkwardly, his head tilted in his fiancée's direction, but his eyes were elsewhere, restless.

They landed on Daisy for a tiny moment and she felt too warm suddenly. What was *that* about? Why was he looking at her now, when he hadn't met her eyes once during their greeting and awkward first conversation? What was wrong with the man?

Or is it something wrong with me?

Everyone was so happy about the wedding. It would be *horrible* if she didn't get along with her sister's husband!

Present Day

In the end, of course, Daisy's feelings about Lee's groom hadn't mattered. The wedding had never taken place. Mom had nagged her a little about the "strong silent type" comment. "You're not suggesting he's not smart enough for her, are you?"

"No, of course not."

"He's cautious, that's all. Sensible, and reserved. And responsible. He thinks before he speaks."

"It's fine, Mom."

"When you get to know him…"

But she never had gotten to know him. Lee and Tucker had announced their decision to call off their wedding just a few days before the scheduled event, both of them looking a little wrung out and sad, but with some relief in the mix at the same time.

For a moment during the announcement, they'd held

hands, but then they'd dropped the contact with two awkward movements that somehow hadn't matched—a sign that the right connection wasn't there, it seemed.

Less than a week later, Daisy had flown out to California, lured by the sudden chance of a three-month internship with an internationally known pastry chef. From then on, far too busy with her fifteen-hour days in a hectic professional kitchen, she'd taken the whole thing at face value whenever she thought back on it.

A mutual decision, announced while standing side by side.

The strong silent type wasn't what Lee wanted, after all.

Now, after what Mary Jane had said this morning, Daisy wondered how much more there'd been to the situation that she hadn't seen at the time.

It was an uncomfortable feeling, like a nagging itch in a place she couldn't reach to scratch. Her phone began to ring. She grabbed it quickly and found it was Lee. "Sorry I missed you. What's up?"

"You sound breathless," Daisy said, relieved to hear her sister's voice. It would be good to get this settled *before* she talked to Tucker himself.

"Just got back from a five-mile run," Lee said.

"You didn't have to call me back before you've even got your breathing back to normal." Except that already it almost was. Lee was incredibly fit.

And although convenient, the timing of her call was a little awkward. "I'm good," she said. "Now, shoot, Daze."

Daisy picked her words carefully. "Look, I'm here at Reid Landscaping…"

"Oh. Wow. You mean Tucker's company?"

"That's right."

"You're thinking of contracting him for the work at Spruce Bay?"

"Yes, only Mary Jane…has doubts."

"Because of me?" Lee had a habit of getting right to the point.

"That's right," she said again, aware that Jackie could overhear.

"That's ridiculous!"

"Well, yes, I thought so, but I wanted to check with you."

"And you've checked, and I'm good, so go ahead."

Daisy laughed. "You are the most efficient conversationalist I know, Lee."

"Only when I'm busting to get into the shower. Seriously, it seems like half a lifetime ago that he and I were planning a big wedding, and I am *sooo* not that kind of girl anymore. If I ever was. Mary Jane is projecting her own stuff."

"Well, yeah, I did wonder about that."

"I was hurt at the time. I mean, I was."

"I don't think I knew that…"

"You were hardly around. But now I know it's the best thing that could have happened, us calling that wedding off. Are we done?"

"We're done. Go take your shower."

They ended the conversation seconds later, just as the phone vibrated on the Reid Landscaping office manager's desk. Jackie checked it quickly and said, "Okay, you're in luck, Ms. Cherry."

"Please call me Daisy."

"Daisy. Such a pretty name!"

"Thanks."

"Tucker can see you now. He'll be coming in from the display area in a moment or two."

"Can I meet him out there?" Daisy jumped up. "I don't want to create too much of an interruption." She felt a little claustrophobic in here for some reason, and suddenly craved the open air with its October crispness and bite.

"Sure, go through the door here," the office manager said. "You'll see him coming across in a minute or two." Once more, there was that flicker of curiosity in Jackie's manner, and Daisy wondered what it meant.

Probably nothing. Curiosity was a natural response. She was feeling it, too. If she'd never gotten to know Tucker Reid ten years ago when he was about to marry her sister, what would she feel about him now?

Would he still be that granite-faced, uncomfortable presence she'd been able to call to memory so clearly a few minutes ago? Would he be someone that carefree Lee would still be happy to think of as a friend? Would he be the man Mary Jane thought he was—cold and superficial enough to dump his fiancée because she had some burn scarring on one side of her lower jaw and neck and shoulder?

Or was there another truth to the man that none of the Cherry sisters had understood?

The paving stones were a delaying tactic. Tucker knew it even as he placed another one in position, rocking it back and forth on its sand foundation to make sure it was steady.

It wasn't.

Or level.

He didn't have the spirit level with him to enable a final adjustment, so he was not just delaying his meeting with Daisy Cherry here, he was actively wasting his own time, because he would probably end up lifting all the pavers and laying them down again from scratch in order to get them right.

He sighed between his teeth, irritated at himself.

And then picked up another paving stone. There was something about physical labor that settled his head. He'd always been that way, through his father's illness, through all the anger and mess, through the years he'd spent filling his dad's shoes too young. When he had something on his mind, he worked through it, literally. Raking leaves in his parents' yard at thirteen. Unloading deliveries at the garden center at twenty.

Or fiddling uselessly with pavers right now.

He didn't like thinking back on his relationship with Lee, that was the problem. And he definitely didn't like thinking about Daisy's part in the whole thing.

No, that wasn't fair.

As far as Daisy herself knew, she hadn't been involved at all.

It was all me.

It had so nearly been a disaster—so very, very nearly—and he couldn't give himself any credit for averting that disaster. He'd seen it coming, but he hadn't been the one to act. He'd let Lee and fate do that. He'd been paralyzed by his intense need to do the right thing, without knowing what the right thing was.

There were reasons for the paralysis, but he found it hard to forgive himself for it all the same.

He sometimes still thought about getting in touch with Lee to see how she was doing. Thought about calling or emailing, but how did you do that? How did you revive something that had started as a friendship and should never have turned into anything else? How did you just ask someone out of the blue, "Hey…are you happy?"

You can ask Lee's sister if Lee is happy. You can ask her today. She would know the answer to that.

But he wasn't convinced that he would manage to frame the question. He could end up holding back and holding back until someone else took the matter into their own hands, the way he had held back ten years ago.

Yeah, he definitely hadn't forgiven himself for that.

Ten years earlier

Something's not right.

The thought was nagging and insistent, prodding at Tucker like someone trying to get his attention with the point of an umbrella. Hey, you! Notice me! Do something!

Everything's not right.

"...and Mom is still questioning the fact that we're only giving chocolate as wedding favors," Lee was saying.

Tucker tried to listen, tried to feel that what his fiancée was saying was important. "I think it's fine," he said, and she nodded, but neither of them was really thinking about chocolate or wedding etiquette or any of that.

I'm thinking I don't want to go ahead with this, and I've known it in my heart for a while, and today it's making me sick. It's like lead in my stomach. It's gotten worse. Oh boy, has it gotten worse! How could this happen? Everyone in both families is so happy about the wedding, I shouldn't be feeling this way.

Was that what Lee was thinking, too? Or was she just scared? Scared because she could see that he was thinking it?

His mind scattered onto six different tracks at once. Scared because she didn't know what he was thinking, because he was fighting so hard not to let it show?

More than that, he was fighting so hard not to feel it.

He honestly did not know if it was just prewedding jitters, the kind everyone had, or if it was a serious problem, and he didn't dare to bare his soul to a listening ear in order to find out. Not to Lee, not to anyone.

Dad had "followed his heart" and left havoc in his wake for years, made his whole family miserable. Tucker thought that human hearts could talk a lot of disastrous nonsense, and had vowed many times that he would keep his where it belonged, under the firm control of his head.

Meanwhile, Daisy had disappeared into the kitchen.

Daisy, who'd knocked him off course the moment he'd set eyes on her from an upstairs bedroom window less than an hour ago. He'd never expected it. How the hell could you *expect* something like that?

He'd heard the car swinging in from the resort driveway to park beside the house, a little later than predicted. Mary Jane had been the one to go pick up Daisy from Albany airport. He'd heard voices—Lee and his future in-laws, Marshall and Denise, as they rushed outside to greet her.

He'd stepped over to the window. Daisy was climbing out of the car. Shafts of afternoon sun struck her blond hair and glinted on earrings and a gold bangle on a bare, lightly tanned wrist. She was wearing jeans, a white top and some kind of pointless but beautiful, vibrantly colorful summery scarf that got mixed up in her huge, warm hug with Lee.

She didn't even seem to see Lee's newly scarred skin, she was just so busy hugging her and exclaiming, wiping happy tears from her eyes, laughing. She hugged her parents, said something about the beautiful June day and the sun on the water.

"You're later than we expected," Denise Cherry said.

"My fault," Daisy answered. "I want to bake for you tonight, so we stopped for ingredients."

"You don't have to bake for us! Not when you're only just home!"

"I want to. Please! I really do!" She was already diving into the trunk of the car and bringing out shopping bags. "I'm going to do a raspberry dacquoise that's so luscious we'll have to row right around the lake to burn off the calories. And a peach tart, because French tarts are just so gorgeous to look at."

"I don't know where you get the energy, honey!"

Tucker didn't know, either. All he knew was that it glowed from every pore of her skin and he was captivated by it. Lee was pretty energetic, too. She liked to hike and ski and climb and run, and he loved that about her—that she was active and fit, and not some girlie girl who wouldn't set foot outdoors for fear of ruining a pedicure.

But Daisy's energy was different, electric and beautiful, and he couldn't take his eyes off her.

He felt as if he was spying, a voyeur, betraying Lee, betraying the whole Cherry family, betraying himself, and even his mother, who adored Lee. And he kept right on doing it, watching the outline and movement of Daisy's body as she carried the shopping bags. She paused to take another look around her at the beloved, familiar sights of home, and let out a big sigh of contentment that he felt in his own body.

It couldn't be happening.

Even if it was happening, it couldn't mean anything, or be important in any way. It was just some stupid symptom of his prewedding nerves. He seriously didn't believe in this kind of thing. He seriously didn't *want* to believe in it, after Dad. And if it seemed to be happening anyway, then it was just a meaningless illusion. It wasn't real.

And yet… He felt it again a little later, when they formally met, the moment they shook hands. The aura of creative energy and star-kissed good fortune that radiated from her like an inner light, the optimism and curiosity and zest for life. Her hair, her eyes, her bow of a mouth, the way she undraped that stupid, beautiful scarf, unconsciously running her hand over the silk as if its color gave off heat and her fingers were cold.

Wow.

Just wow.

There were three Cherry sisters in his life. He liked the eldest one a lot, even though she could be prickly at times and he couldn't stand Alex, her boyfriend. He loved the middle one like a comrade-in-arms and he was going to marry her. He *was*. Everyone wanted it.

Sister number three was a revelation he hadn't expected or wanted or—

Hadn't wanted.

Really, really didn't want.

He wanted to marry Lee.

He wanted to *want* to marry Lee.

"Should we get out of here?" she asked him suddenly, and he realized he was still staring into space, roughly in the direction of the kitchen door, even though it was a good forty-five seconds since Daisy had disappeared through it.

"Out of here?" he echoed stupidly.

"Away," Lee said. "Right after dinner. Go to a bar, or something. Even better, skip dinner and go to a bar right now."

"You know we can't do that." As a future Cherry son-in-law…as the *first* future Cherry son-in-law…he was well aware of family requirements five days before the wedding, and his sense of duty about it was strong. "Not even after dinner."

"Is it wrong that I want to?" There was a huge amount of appeal in Lee's voice, and he didn't know how to answer her.

"We're both on edge." He touched her neck. It was a caress he'd used countless times before the accident and he wasn't out of the habit of it yet, even though he knew she didn't like it anymore. The burn scarring there and on her jaw and shoulder was fading now, but it was still too fresh for comfort and would never fully disappear, and they were both self-conscious about it, second-guessing their own motivations.

Was he only touching her neck to prove that he didn't mind touching it? Did she only dislike it because she didn't believe such a caress could possibly be sincere? She hated the scarring way more than he did.

Why had he started touching her neck in the first place? He liked her so much, they were such great friends, they had things in common, but that slightly crazy party night when friendship had spilled over into something physical...

To be honest, he wondered where they would be now if that night had never happened.

Maybe we would have stayed just friends, and I would have met Daisy instead...

No! Idiot!

When Lee had still been in the hospital after the accident, they'd both said to each other that this was what love was all about, going through the dark times together as well as the good times, and yet...

Something's not right.

It wasn't just wedding jitters.

And it wasn't just Daisy.

Lee felt it, too, he was sure she did.

Almost sure.

But she wasn't saying anything.

And he couldn't say it for her because then she'd think…everyone would think…that he was doing it because of the accident, when really he thought the accident had done him a favor, reaffirming his bone-deep understanding of how serious marriage was, forcing a realization that they weren't together for the right reasons. They cared about each other, but not in the right way.

I have to say it. If she won't, I have to.

But what if he was wrong? What if this was just a temporary blip in the beat of his untrustworthy heart? What if the Reid and Cherry families were right to be so happy about the wedding? And what if Lee was devastated instead of relieved? Could he do that to her?

He couldn't say it. Was there any way he could work out what both of them really felt without resorting to the finality of words? Maybe the best marriages were the ones that started out exactly the way he'd started out with Lee—as friends. After seeing what passion and wild impulse had done to his own family, he truly didn't think that was the way to go.

So where did Daisy fit in?

She didn't, his own ruthless honesty told him. He'd schooled himself not to believe in rosy scenarios, after Dad's lymphoma diagnosis and his reaction to it. Life wasn't sunny and effortless. Life wasn't about going where the winds of emotion blew you. Life was struggle. Given a choice between believing in easy miracles and believing in solid work, Tucker chose the hard yards every time.

Daisy didn't fit. Daisy was an illusion.

She was oblivious, and it was better that way.

"You're right," he told Lee. "After dinner. After we've

put in as much time as anyone could expect. We do need to get out of here and get a couple of hours to ourselves."

"Or I'm going to explode."

"Me, too."

"We need to talk, and—"

"Yes, work things out. Think. Out loud. To each other." The words didn't come easily. Frustrated by the difficulty of coherent speech, he grabbed her shoulders and squeezed her and felt the breath come out of her as if she'd been holding it for too long. She squeezed him back.

"Yes. Yes. We really do," she said, and blinked back what could have been tears.

Shoot, he was giddy with relief!

Giddy, and thirsty, he realized. He'd been out of doors from six until two at the garden center, where he worked three days a week on top of his hours at the hotel. He'd repotted grafted plants, unloaded new stock and supplies, planned his own future landscaping business inside his head while his body lifted and carried and stacked and sorted. He'd grabbed a burger and a sugar-filled soda for lunch, but hadn't had a real, thirst-quenching drink since before noon.

Thinking only of a long glass of clear, icy mountain water, he made for the kitchen, and there was Daisy stirring a pot that bubbled with sweet, fragrant syrup. He could smell it the moment he walked in.

And the moment he walked in, he was far too aware of her—of how pretty and exotic she seemed, so freshly arrived from France, with that indefinable nuance of Frenchness about her. She looked a little steamy at the hot stove, with pink in her cheeks and several tendrils of fine, golden-blond hair curling around her face in the humid warmth. She brushed one back behind her ear then looked up and caught sight of him.

They looked at each other.

He froze inside and looked away before either of them could even blink.

This was *not important.* This was *not* what was making him jittery about his future with Lee. The jitters had been building for weeks, when Daisy was just a name and a vague reference.

He'd seen her in family pictures as a cute toddler and then a gangly-limbed teen, and right up until their meeting ten minutes ago he'd still been thinking of her as a kid, as Lee's kid sister.

Someone he might tease a little about boyfriends.

Someone *with* a boyfriend—a local guy she'd known since high school who'd been texting and calling and emailing her faithfully the whole year she was in France.

She didn't have a boyfriend, he'd learned.

Not that this was important, either way.

But still, they'd looked at each other for that tiny moment before he'd flinched his gaze away.

"Thirsty," he said, to explain his presence.

"Beer or soda?" she offered, smiling. "There's both in the refrigerator."

"Actually, water..."

"Bottled or tap?"

"Tap is fine. I'll help myself."

"Thanks. I can't leave this glaze right now, or very bad things will happen to it."

"No problem." He ran the faucet, and cold mountain water gushed into his glass. And then he took it outside to drink it, because he didn't trust himself to stay anywhere near her.

Chapter Three

Present Day

Out in the yard, Daisy saw Tucker in worn jeans and a plaid flannel shirt with the sleeves rolled up his arms the same way—although it was not the same shirt—as they'd been in the photo on the wall inside.

He was shifting a large paving stone into place in an open-air alcove that formed one of Reid Landscaping's displays. There were five of these alcoves, each designed to show what could be achieved with barbecue areas, ponds and fountains, raised garden beds and a dozen other features.

He straightened, stepped back to judge his work and was apparently satisfied. He paused for a moment to stretch his shoulders and check his phone, then turned to begin striding across the large yard, sliding the phone into his back pocket as he caught sight of her. She waved at him and came forward to meet him before he got too close to the building. She really didn't want to end up back inside, with the possibility of their conversation being overheard.

Just in case Mary Jane was right about the kind of person he was—the nasty kind, like Mary Jane's ex. After her long experience with Alex Stewart, maybe Mary Jane was a really good judge of scumbag men. Maybe there really was a good reason, even after all this time, *not* to contract Tucker's company to relandscape the Spruce Bay grounds, and it was all bound up in Lee's accident and Tucker's response.

Daisy wondered again about the second reason, the one Mary Jane hadn't spoken.

The one that had put a stubborn, shuttered look onto her face, as if the second reason was something she wouldn't confess even under torture.

Tucker saw her and stopped to wait until she reached him, watching her with a steadiness that unnerved her, given how uncomfortable she was already feeling. Those memories of his unreadable presence ten years ago were fresher and more vivid than they should have been.

She hadn't been too impressed with strong and silent back then, but she'd learned to appreciate it in the years since, and the Tucker Reid of today was even more impressive in the flesh than he'd been in the photos on the main office wall, hard and solid and strong, with the kind of maleness that only belongs to a man who works hard with his body in the open air.

Daisy knew she would be incredibly disappointed if she couldn't manage to like him, if he was exactly what Mary Jane claimed him to be, or worse.

Superficial. Unkind. A womanizer. All of the above.

"Daisy," he said when she was close enough. He gave

her a brief smile, but it didn't last. She started to hold out
her hand, but he turned his palm up and showed the dirt
and they both gave an awkward shrug and dropped the
idea. "It's been a while."

"It has."

"Jackie says you'd rather talk out here?"

"Oh, she—?"

"Sent a text about ten seconds ago. Weird how we do
things now, isn't it?" Most people would probably have
smiled with that line, but he didn't.

"Weird…" Daisy echoed. "Convenient."

"Want to sit here?" he offered. "It's a sun trap. Beautiful today. Better than inside."

"That's what I thought." He wasn't giving her much,
she decided. Short phrases, an offhand observation about
phones. Their exchange seemed familiar, a flashback to
their brief acquaintance in the past.

She settled herself a little stiffly on the wide wooden
bench seat he'd indicated. In a sheltered, sunny position it
was warm to the touch even in October, and the splash of
an ornamental fountain nearby brought a sense of natural
tranquility that contrasted uncomfortably with the rather
less peaceful feelings inside her.

*Who were we back then, all of us? Mary Jane, and Lee,
and Tucker, and me? What's Mary Jane not telling me?
Why am I feeling so tense about this, now that I'm here?*

"What can I do for you today?" Tucker asked, sitting
down beside her. He kept to his own body space, their
hips a good two feet apart, with a safe stretch of smooth,
sunny bench in between. Did they really need that?

"You mean because I'm actually supposed to be meeting you tomorrow at the resort?"

He shrugged and smiled. The smile was too tight. "I
guess that's what I'm asking."

Suddenly, she realized that she didn't know how to handle this. It had seemed easy on her way here, but maybe it wasn't going to be.

Face-to-face, with Tucker understandably expecting her to take the initiative since this meeting was her idea, she felt her poise evaporate like spilled water on hot pavement. She couldn't exactly accuse him of breaking up with her sister for nasty reasons ten years ago, and then ask him if he was still the same kind of man.

And yet she had to say something, or he wouldn't know why she was here.

With no other option, in the end she just said it the best she could. "Mary Jane thinks it's inappropriate for Spruce Bay Resort to hire Reid Landscaping for the work on our grounds because you were once engaged to our sister."

"Ah," he said.

Which gave her just about as much as he'd given her ten years ago—one handshake, a few words and a couple of looks that disappeared too fast.

She waited for more.

After a moment, it came, but it wasn't much help. "And what do you think?" He shifted a little on the bench. Farther away, not closer. Still, the movement made her more aware of him, of just how strong and solid he was, of just how well those jeans fit his muscled legs. He was intimidating.

"I—I didn't think it should be a problem. Which was why I set up the appointment without consulting her first."

"You didn't think it should be a problem. But now you do?" He'd narrowed his eyes against the bright light, but the glint of blue was still strong. She was very glad not to know exactly what he might be thinking.

"No, I—" she began, then stopped and started again. "Well, I just thought we should explore the idea. Mary

Jane is pretty sensible…" She gathered herself and sat up straighter, determined to take a little more control of the conversation. "Seriously, though, on this occasion I think she's wrong. I've also talked to Lee on the phone, and she says she's fine about it. But still, I thought we should get it out in the open. You were engaged to Lee, and then the wedding got canceled. I want Reid Landscaping because I know you're the best in the area, and I don't see that having a personal connection so long ago is going to be an issue. I want to be able to reassure Mary Jane that you and I have talked about it and dealt with any concerns."

He was silent for a moment, and she wondered if this meant he thought the same way as Mary Jane. Then he took a deep breath. "Tell me how Lee is," he finally said. "She's still in Colorado? Is she married? Kids?" He took another breath. "Is she happy?"

This was easy, thank goodness. "She's still in Colorado. Yes, she's really happy. I don't think marriage and kids figure on her agenda."

"No?" He slid her a sideways glance.

"That's what she says. I've visited her there a couple times. From what I can see, she has everything set up just the way she wants, and she's not pining for change."

"That's good," he answered. "That's really great."

"Well, we all think so, yes."

"Meaning it's none of my business because I took myself out of her life at the wrong time?"

"That's Mary Jane, not me," she said quickly.

"Mary Jane thinks it was my fault, you mean, that the wedding got called off?"

"Apparently."

"Mary Jane needs to find something better to do with her time than making judgments about something that happened so long ago," Tucker growled, and it was so close to what Daisy had just been thinking that she almost groaned out loud.

"It won't be a problem," she said quickly. "She's going to Africa tomorrow."

"Africa?"

"She loves to travel. She'll be gone for three weeks. I mean, I'm not sure how booked up your schedule is..."

"Pretty booked up."

"Right."

"I'll see what I can squeeze in. You mean, if we could have the design and budget and timetable all locked in by the time she gets back, she'd realize everything had been worked out with no difficulties?"

"I'd been wondering if you might even have started on the actual work by then."

Ah. No.

"Not possible, I'm afraid." The look he gave her clearly said, *Reid Landscaping is way more in demand than you realize,* and she was embarrassed at being caught out in such a mistaken assumption. It seemed arrogant on her part, entitled, and she was quite horrified about how well he could get his meaning across without words.

She backpedaled politely, aware that this improvised meeting had not achieved very much. She'd been too impulsive in coming here, hadn't thought it through. "In that case, if we're lucky enough to have an estimate and plans by then, that would be great."

"So I can leave you with Jackie, then?" He didn't try to hide that he needed to end this meeting. In fact, he was so cool about it that she wondered if he wanted Spruce Bay's business at all.

She stood, and said even more politely than before, "Of course, since you're busy."

He closed his eyes for a moment, then let out a sigh between his teeth. "I'm sorry, that sounded rude."

"You *are* busy."

"Jackie's been with us since we started. She knows more than I do about prices and delivery times, and she has a great eye. I have an appointment I need to get to. Shouldn't have sounded so impatient about it. Sorry."

"It's fine."

He smiled, and she felt a rush of relief that the intimidating distance seemed to have shrunk to a much more manageable level. "You can have a browse around here," he offered. He made a gesture of casual ownership that hinted at his sense of success. "Take a look through our gallery of past projects and gather some ideas, get Jackie to show you the brochures from our suppliers."

"Sounds good. Please go to your appointment and leave me to it, and we'll meet as planned at Spruce Bay tomorrow."

"Looking forward to it."

But he wasn't. She could see it in the guarded expression that had appeared again on his face, and she didn't know why it was there.

Ten years earlier

"We have to pick up the tuxes from the hire place," Lee said to Tucker in their usual corner of their usual bar, "finalize the seating arrangements and write out the place cards, work out the checks we're going to need to give to people on the day and write those out. We should probably call the hotel to confirm our reservations—"

"Lee," Tucker cut in quietly. "Is this really why you wanted to get away and talk? To go through our to-do list for the millionth time? We can talk about this stuff anywhere."

She got that frightened, doubtful look on her face. "But we weren't talking just now, were we? We weren't saying anything. I was…filling the silence."

"There's allowed to be silence, isn't there?"

"Not when—" She stopped and took a breath, lifted her strong chin. She had the strongest face of the three Cherry girls, determined and full of courage. Tucker was so grateful that the burning oil hadn't splashed more than an inch above her jawline to change those contoured planes. She began again. "Not when all I can think about when we're silent is that I can almost feel you wanting to call this off."

"Call it off," he echoed blankly, as if he didn't know.

"Yes. Cancel. End it. Tell me it's been a mistake. I keep waiting for you to say it, and you don't."

"Because I didn't want to hurt—" *Wrong, wrong, wrong.*

Her eyes narrowed and she went white. "That's why? *That's* why? I thought you might not be sure about what you were feeling. Wedding jitters. I'm having them, too, and the other stuff, the sense that we're not connecting, and I haven't known if it was temporary— But now you're saying— You're telling me you *knew* this wasn't right, knew it for sure, but you were just going to go ahead with it anyhow?"

"Not for sure. I was— I kept—" But he couldn't say it. He didn't really know, himself, what he'd been going to do. He didn't feel as if he understood anything right now. He kept thinking about his dad, and his own determination never to do anything even remotely similar to what he had done. You had to consider your family's happiness, not just your own. You couldn't let your emotions blow you every which way like leaves in the wind.

She said it for him. "You were going to *marry* me, be-cause you didn't want to *hurt my feelings*. Do you have *any* idea how insulting that is?"

It went downhill from there.

And then, eventually, after quite a long time, with a lot of silence, some tears, some words, it came partway back up. "It's a relief," Lee said quietly. "I'm relieved."

But when they got back to the house she didn't even wait for him to kill the engine before she jumped out of the car, gabbled something he couldn't catch and disap-peared inside. By the time he reached the porch, he could hear through the open front door her feet clattering up the stairs toward the privacy of her room.

He didn't go inside.

He couldn't. Not yet.

He needed some space. They'd decided not to say any-thing to anyone else until tomorrow. "Daisy only arrived six hours ago," Lee had said. "I don't want to hit everyone with this news until she's settled in a little."

"It's not about Daisy, is it?" he'd answered, and the words had felt like a lie in his mouth.

Was it about Daisy?

Hell, he definitely wasn't going inside right now, be-cause Daisy would probably be there.

He sat on the porch steps instead, hunching over to rest his elbows on his spread knees and brooding in the dark. A slew of different emotions roiled inside him, as choppy and confusing as the waves on the lake when the weather was changing.

This whole thing felt like a change in the weather, a change in the season. That unsettling feeling at the end of summer when the leaves rattled down from the trees in a sudden wind, and the temperature dropped forty de-

car. Could you grab it for me and toss it up? Is it locked, Mary Jane?" she called a little louder.

Mary Jane cleared her throat, and called back, "No, it's open. I can get it for you."

"But I bet Tucker can throw better than you."

"I could *bring* it up to you, Daisy," Mary Jane said tetchily, starting across the porch and down the steps. "Nobody has to *throw* it!"

"I got it," Tucker said quickly. The car was parked only yards away. He found the hairbrush on the front dash and held it up for Daisy to see. "You really want me to...?"

"Sure, why not." She reached out for it. He threw it neatly, and she caught it even more neatly, laughing.

He thought he would remember that moment for the rest of his life.

Present Day

And he did, damn it, he still remembered it.

Abandoning the crooked paving stones, he went out the side entrance to his car, parked in its designated space at the front of the private parking lot, while Daisy began to browse the display areas. He could see her as he sat in the vehicle waiting for the engine to warm, in her bright blue biker-style jacket and black pants. She walked slowly, pausing every time something caught her attention.

She stepped back to appreciate the effect of the morning sun on the splashing water of a fountain, stepped forward again to run her hand across a piece of blue-gray slate. She picked up a glazed black pot planted with miniature bamboo and set it on the slate as if testing the blend of colors, and then she put it carefully back exactly where she'd found it.

This was what had drawn him so strongly ten years

ago—the intensity of her response to beauty, the creative energy that ran through her, the bright light she seemed to give off, when the darkness of his father's illness and its aftermath had still been hanging over him.

The car engine was warm. He had no reason to still be sitting here. He had to take himself off before she noticed...except that her browsing made her oblivious, the way she'd been oblivious that very first day.

The one thing he could be proud of, possibly. He'd kept his cataclysmic thunderclap of feeling to himself.

Lee hadn't guessed. Marshall and Denise had had no idea. They'd gotten it all wrong. Marshall had accosted him in the privacy of the resort office after all the phone calls had been made—canceling the reception, the photographer, the flowers, the guests.

"I cannot believe you're doing this, Tucker. My incredibly brave, beautiful girl is pretending she wants it, too, but I'm not fooled. This is coming from you. Maybe she doesn't even know that. Maybe she genuinely thinks this is a mutual decision, but I've seen you withdrawing over the past few weeks. You've frozen her out until she thinks it's coming from her, as well. I know what a man looks like when he's truly in love with the woman he's going to marry. You haven't looked that way, and if it's because my girl is disfigured after the—"

"Marshall, she's not—" He hadn't been able to say it. *Disfigured.* He'd never said that in his head, never felt that way.

"You don't want that word? It's too blunt for you?" Marshall had used it as a punishment and an accusation. "You don't like facing the truth about your own motivations?"

It hadn't been a pleasant conversation, and Tucker had come dangerously close to saying Daisy's name but he'd managed to stop himself, and if that meant that Marshall went on thinking that it was Lee's accident at the heart of the problem, then this was collateral damage that he couldn't avoid.

He didn't want Daisy dragged into this. He didn't want any additional hurt to Lee, or a mess worse than the mess they had already.

He would wait, he had decided. He would just lay low and do nothing, and in a few months when things had died down and when he had some perspective, he would take action, seek Daisy out, see if he still felt…and if she felt…and if there was any way they could possibly…

Hadn't happened.

He drove out of the lot, remembering the shock he'd felt when he'd run into a very bubbly Daisy at a local convenience store just a few days after the canceled wedding. Hiding his pleasure behind dark sunglasses, he'd drawled, "You're looking happy today."

She'd told him, "Happy and really thrilled. I'm flying out to California tomorrow to start an internship with an amazing pastry chef. The opportunity came up so fast, I haven't had time to breathe! Someone else canceled, and it turned out I was second on the list. I can't believe it! Um…it's good to see you, Tucker, but I have to run."

And that was that.

Gone.

He'd never pursued it. Why would he trust in signs that pointed in two different directions at once, when he didn't believe in signs in the first place? Why would he chase after something his head didn't even want? Something that might only ever have been a symptom of the deeper problem between himself and Lee? Something nobody in either family would want? Something that fate had chosen to take out of his hands?

"Ten years later…" he muttered to himself as he drove.

Ten years later, incredibly, he'd felt exactly the same. Thunderclap. Across a crowded landscape display. Changing everything.

Magic.

Chemistry.

Whatever you wanted to call it.

It was just as strong, and he distrusted it just as much. He'd hidden it manfully during their brief meeting today, and he didn't think she'd guessed. He hoped she hadn't, because his beliefs and his morals were still the same, and this feeling about Daisy wasn't something he believed in or wanted to pursue.

Not with his legacy of experience, and not with his current situation the way it was.

You see, there was a little thing called a marriage certificate, and call him old-fashioned, but, no matter what the circumstances, he didn't think a man should go after one woman when he was already legally wed to someone else.

Chapter Four

"So I saw your half brother today," Tucker's mother, Nancy, told him that night.

She'd called him to see if he could come over and fix a leak in the U-bend pipe beneath the kitchen sink and change the lightbulb at the top of the stairs. At sixty-one years old, she was pretty good about most of that stuff.

He was proud of her, actually. She mowed her own lawn, changed all the lightbulbs she could reach, paid her bills on time. He'd in fact forbidden her to change the one at the top of the stairs, since it involved climbing onto a chair and leaning precariously into space.

With a trim, energetic figure and hair she'd allowed to remain its natural silvery gray, she could have married again if she'd wanted to, Tucker was certain, and yet to his knowledge she'd never come close. A couple times he'd almost asked her about it—*"Did you love Dad that* much?" Or maybe, *"Did Dad scar you that badly?"* But in the end he'd stayed silent.

"Oh, you did?" he said to her carefully now, about Jonah.

"He's working at Third Central, the branch on the corner of Maple and Twenty-second Street, and I had checks to deposit," Mom explained. "I don't usually go to that branch, but I had a delivery down that way." She had her own business as a florist now, having started in that field as a sales assistant after his dad became ill. "He's looking so grown-up, I guess he'd be twenty-one by now."

"About that, I think."

"He didn't recognize me." She added, "Or if he did, he was pretending, the same way I was."

There wasn't much else to say. Jonah had been three years old at their dad's funeral, a difficult imp of a kid who didn't understand what was happening. Tucker's mom had been horrified that Andrea would bring him. *How could she do this?* she'd said over and over. *How could she do this?*

She'd been devastated at Andrea's presence, exhausted by the effort of dealing with it. Jonah crying and struggling in his mother's arms had been the last straw on top of more previous last straws than Tucker could count.

His mom had found out about his dad's affair three months after she'd learned about his cancer. Three months after that, she'd found out that the woman involved was eight months pregnant with Dad's child.

But the order she'd found out about it wasn't the order in which it had all happened. Dad had known he was ill months before he'd told his family, and he'd started the affair almost immediately "as a reaction." The justification he'd used still made Tucker queasy with anger. *I had to follow my guiding star. I had to go with how I felt. Me, not anyone else. I had to live life to the full, while I still had the chance.*

That's not how you react, Dad. Cancer is supposed to bring you closer to the people who love you, not send you off on a self-absorbed wild-goose chase for your lost youth.

Yeah.

What did you say about all that, eighteen years after Dad was gone?

"It's not Jonah's fault," Mom said, as she'd said before, and it was true.

She'd talked a lot, at one time, about getting to know him. "He looks so much like you and Mattie when you were that age, Tucker."

But it was impossible. There was still too much anger and mess, no possibility of any forgiveness between Andrea Lewers and his mom. His mom blamed Andrea for the affair because she couldn't cope with blaming his dad. Andrea blamed his mom for shutting her out and dismissing her grief because somehow she'd loved his dad, too.

In the end, Tucker had steered his mother away from the idea of making any kind of connection with his half brother, and so they barely knew him. They knew him from a distance because Mom hadn't been able to stop herself from keeping track of him.

"You didn't go to that branch because you knew he was working there, did you?" Tucker accused gently.

She looked at him and sighed. "No, I didn't. I've been so good about that these past couple years. No, it was a total coincidence. You're right in what you've always said. Too much mess, and Jonah himself doesn't need to be dumped in it."

"I really think that's the only way to go." He felt a wash of relief on realizing that he didn't have to argue the case.

"Speaking of mess, though…" his mom said.

"Yeah? Are we?"

She took a breath, a certain very mothery kind of breath. "Emma called a couple days ago, and we had a talk."

"Oh, you did?" His wariness kicked in.

When his mom brought Emma into the conversation, the result was rarely a relaxing chat. Her manner turned plaintive, and she couldn't hold herself back. "Tucker, I don't think she wants this divorce, and I don't understand why the two of you haven't tried harder."

He sighed. "Because that wasn't the agreement. You know that."

"You can rethink the agreement. I think that's what she wants, at heart. For you to work at it and turn it into a real marriage, instead of just letting it go."

"No, she doesn't. She really doesn't, Mom."

She ignored him. "You could have such a great partnership. Everyone would be so happy about it. You've had a broken engagement, and now a marriage that isn't what it could be. I'm not sure what it is that you want. I don't understand why—"

"I think you're wrong."

"About the marriage, or about what Emma wants?"

"Both. It's not like she and I haven't talked about this."

"She's scared to say it. She needs it to come from you."

"No, Mom. We've been married three years. If there was any possibility of it turning into the real thing, it would have happened by now. There's no chemistry and there never has been."

"Chemistry? You get on so well together…"

"Because we've given each other plenty of space. Because we've been clear about the whole arrangement."

"Emma wants the arrangement to change," she said

firmly, then added as a signal that she wasn't going to keep on about it. "Now, are you staying for coffee and a bite to eat? I have cake."

"Sure, I have time. That would be nice."

When he'd finished the coffee and cake that his mom had pressed on him and they'd talked about Carla and Mattie, and how well they were both doing in New York City, and how it would be nice if one or both of them moved back closer, as well as easy things like TV shows and the weather, he left with that familiar sense of having hosed down a potential emotional crisis.

Or two of them.

His marriage, and Jonah.

Although this wasn't fair, because his mom had changed the subject pretty fast both times, and when it came to action rather than talk, she'd behaved as sensibly and decently about Dad's affair and Tucker's own unusual marriage as she possibly could.

And that was exactly the way he was going to behave about Daisy Cherry. Sensible and decent.

Maybe it was good that his mom had run into Jonah today. It gave Tucker a very necessary reminder of how much he hated complicated, emotionally messy entanglements. Giving in to an attraction to his ex-fiancée's sister while his green-card marriage was still a legal reality was quite a bit more complicated and messy than he wanted.

Chapter Five

Their mom and dad were driving Mary Jane down to Albany to catch her connecting flight to Newark airport first thing on Tuesday morning. Mary Jane and Daisy had a big, squeezy goodbye hug, and neither of them said a word about yesterday's argument, Tucker Reid or the work required on the Spruce Bay grounds.

"Have a great time in Africa!"

"Oh, I'll try… I will!"

Tucker arrived for the scheduled meeting at just about the time Mary Jane would be boarding her aircraft, and since their mom and dad were stopping for lunch in Saratoga on their way home, he would be long gone by the time they got back.

Possibly a good thing.

Mom and Dad were bowing out of the family business and had decided on South Carolina, "so we don't keep interfering with what you girls want to do with the place," but they hadn't made the move yet, and they did interfere. A lot. With profuse apologies every single time.

Daisy didn't want Tucker caught in the middle of family stuff. After all, he hadn't been a part of the Cherry family for a long time.

At two minutes before ten, she heard the metallic slam of a heavy vehicle door and peeked out the office window to see a juggernaut of a pickup truck parked out front, with the blue-and-green Reid Landscaping logo emblazoned on the side. She neatened the sheaf of printouts and brochures she'd taken from Jackie at the landscaping office yesterday, and slid her own hand-written notes into the folder, as well.

She liked having a folder, and notes. They were practical and impersonal and gave emphasis to the working nature of this relationship. They were a reminder of how she used to clutch a pile of menus at Niche, after her professional and personal relationship with head chef and owner Michael Drake had gone downhill.

Shoot, she hated even thinking about it, but she couldn't stop herself sometimes!

She'd fallen for him hard, from almost their first meeting nearly two years ago. Working so hard to establish herself as a pastry chef, she'd rarely had time for dating, and a serious relationship was long overdue. She was ripe and ready and there he was.

He'd charmed her, lavished her with romantic gestures. It had been the perfect relationship. She remembered calling Lee one night in Colorado and gushing to her about it. "Oh, Lee, I never knew I could feel this way. It's like a fairy tale. They say nothing in life is perfect, but this… this really is."

Too perfect.

Overwhelmingly perfect.

Fake perfect.

She'd quickly gone from being dazzled by the flowers, the phone calls, the smiles-just-for-her, the candlelit dinners and the public parading of their intimacy, to feeling uneasy about the reality of what lay beneath. The stars faded from her eyes and cracks appeared in the facade, revealing a massive ego, no sense of humor and a tendency to turn cold and angry for days if she didn't froth with appreciation and gratitude at his every gesture.

She'd fallen out of love as fast as she'd fallen into it, and felt so foolish, embarrassed and angry at herself for mistaking romantic gestures and sheer lust for the real thing. She'd broken it off, and that was what he couldn't handle, it had turned out. In his world, Michael Drake was always the one to do the dumping.

She'd told him it needn't and wouldn't make a difference to their professional relationship and he'd agreed, but the agreement was as superficial as the romance had been. In fact, he'd undermined her at the restaurant from that moment on, sometimes subtly, sometimes blatantly, depending on how distracted he was by his latest conquest.

She'd waited for him to lose interest in the ugly game of punishment, thinking that if she just kept her head down for long enough, she could ride it out, but he didn't forget and he didn't forgive, and the atmosphere in the kitchen at Niche eventually wore her down too much. She'd suspected, too, that Michael was poisoning her reputation behind her back, so that getting another job in a San Francisco restaurant at the right level would be a challenge.

The whole debacle had made her question the meaning of her life in California. What was really important? What did she want? Where did she see herself in five years or ten? It had been a major factor in her decision to come back to Spruce Bay, and she still combed through those early days with Michael in search of signs she'd missed, and reassurance that she wouldn't make the same mistake with a man again.

Which brought her back full circle to the present, and Tucker Reid.

They met in the open air, as they'd done yesterday. She came out of the office with her clutch of papers to find Tucker paused beside his pickup, surveying the scene from behind dark sunglasses. His gaze pivoted slowly from the overgrown greenery bordering the access road, to the flat semicircle of mown grass in front of the two wings of motel units, to the unshaded rectangle of the pool.

She knew what he would think. "You're right, it's dated and tired," she said so that he didn't have to say it for her.

He turned, hair glinting darkly in the midmorning sun. He was dressed in jeans and a navy polo shirt embroidered in blue and green with his company name and logo. It wasn't really the weather for short sleeves anymore, but he didn't seem aware of the chill in the shade. "Hi... Sorry, was I that easy to read?" he said.

For once, yes!

"It's what anyone would think," she answered honestly. "Mom and Dad were daunted by the idea of a big remodel, so they kept putting it off. It's way past due."

"Happens a lot, especially in a family business." He leaned in through the open window of his truck, grabbed an electronic tablet and clicked it on.

She couldn't stop herself from sighing. "I just don't think they even see some of it. The whole place is too familiar to them." It was a problem Mary Jane had been battling with for some time. "I've done a spreadsheet of our occupancy rates for the past seven years and there's been a perceptible dip. This past season it tailed off even more, and I don't think that's just down to the economy."

He nodded back, fingers moving over the screen. His hands were rough and strong and tanned. Callused, probably. "In fact, when people vacation at a place like this, the last thing they want is to be reminded of a downturn by outdated facilities."

"You're right."

"Show me," Tucker said. He looked up at last. "Show me the areas you think most need work. It's jumping the gun to get to budget details right away, but an idea of your priorities would still help. I'm not going to bring this thing with me." He held up the tablet. "Can I just input a few basics to start? Then I'll leave it in the office and we'll fill in some more after the tour. And maybe you should leave your notes behind, too?"

He gave a quick, unsmiling glance at the overly thick wad of papers and folders, and their protective value shriveled to nothing. Daisy felt strange and awkward and almost *naked* in a way she didn't understand. "If you think we won't need them yet, then sure, yes," she said.

"I'd rather hear your vision, even if it's vague."

One smile, Tucker. How hard would that be?

"So can I leave this in your office?" he asked when he was done with the tablet.

"Let me." She took it and was back a moment later to find the toe of his work boot prodding the partly rotted wooden edging of a garden bed out front, where the shrubs were either stringy and overgrown or half-dead. On an impulse, she asked him with too much need in her voice, "Are we kidding ourselves?"

He began carefully, "You mean…?"

"To think that this place can be brought back to life. There's so much needs doing. Should we be selling it so that some big corporation can bulldoze the whole thing and start from scratch?"

She hated even saying it. She cared so much about this place. More than she'd realized when she left California, she wanted Spruce Bay to be golden and fresh again, and she wanted to be a part of making that happen.

She looked around—at the sparkling glimpses of the lake between the cabins and through the trees, at the separate restaurant building with its wooden deck poised almost over the water, at the aqua blue of the pool, locked away in its boring rectangle of child-safe fencing. The pool *definitely* needed work.

Tucker was watching her. "Do you want to sell it?" he asked, gentle and blunt at the same time.

"No, not at all." She blinked back sudden tears. "I think that would devastate Mom and Dad and Mary Jane."

"What about Lee?"

"Lee would feel she doesn't have the right to insist on us keeping the place when she's not involved in running it, but in her heart, yes, I think she'd hate to see it sold."

"And you?" He seemed to be studying her intently, but she couldn't be sure, with his eyes hidden behind those sunglasses.

"I'd hate it, too. I really love it here. I'd forgotten that. It's where I learned how much beauty means to me. It's where I first started dabbling in a restaurant kitchen, and realized how much I loved to bake and cook. It's where I found out how to power my plans with my dreams."

He was silent, still studying her, and she didn't know where to look, so just kept on with her mental inventory of the familiar sights around her. The playground area, the barbecues, the indoor-games room, and the boat dock and the little crescent of beach that she couldn't actually see from here but could picture so clearly in her mind.

"I think you can make it work," he said after a long moment. "Not everyone could. Not everyone has anything like the—" He stopped and began again. "But yeah, I think you can have the vision you want for Spruce Bay. In fact, I know you can, Daisy Cherry."

She believed him.

Believed in his assurance to a crazy extent, when she thought about it. They'd barely begun to talk budget and plans, and hadn't started their tour. They were just standing here beside a flower bed that should have been stripped out, freshly edged, filled with new soil and re-planted at least six years ago.

"Talk to me," he invited her softly. "If you could do anything at all, what would it be?"

Before she could answer, he began to step across the slightly rutted and weedy gravel of the main driveway, in the direction of the pool. She followed him, measuring grand, dazzling possibilities in her head and not liking what she saw. If it was too grand and dazzling, it wouldn't be Spruce Bay.

"I don't want luxury purely for the sake of it," she said. "I don't want to put this place beyond the reach of regular families and hardworking couples. It doesn't need marble and granite underfoot, bathrooms with gold-plated fittings or landscaping that requires five full-time garden staff."

"No?"

"It just needs to celebrate what it is. The pool and the playground both need to be more enticing." She went in that direction, stepping off the driveway and crossing the unkempt grass because there was no path. "There need to be walkways to draw people to the pool and barbecues, and down to the lake." She quickened her pace. "Everything is just *there*. Dumped with no thought by whoever planned it."

"That wasn't your parents?"

"No, the place was already fifteen years old when they

bought it. But look. Walking tracks are just rutted into the grass. The pool fence looks like it should have a row of Dumpsters inside it. Nothing pulls you where you'd want to go."

She kept going, thinking out loud, calling back to him. "And the trees and shrubs are too overgrown. I wish the restaurant deck had access on this side so people could move more easily between it and the pool. A lot of people don't even realize it has that beautiful deck over the water. I wish the pool was a better shape, not a plain old rectangle."

She turned again toward it, where there were just the four unimaginative rectangles of blue water, a gray concrete surround, green grass surrounding that, and then metal fence around the whole lot.

"I guess back in the sixties when this was first built... before my parents bought it in the late seventies...people didn't think so much about landscaping, but now..." A sweep of her hands filled in the rest, because he had to know what she meant. It was pretty obvious. "We need a new pool, and beyond that, I don't know how much you can achieve just through garden beds and plantings, but if you can, that's what we want. Some magic. Some imagination."

She turned to him, having run out of steam—well, temporarily—and found him standing several yards away with his hands pushed down into the pockets of his jeans, just nodding, quiet in contrast to her rush of words and movement.

A moment ago, he might have been smiling. She caught the last bit of it, caught his firm mouth settling into stillness, the way she sometimes used to catch the last few moments of sunset in California before the start of the dinner rush.

Those glowing glimpses of color used to seem like a secret treat, snatched from the middle of hours of hard work, and his smile seemed the same—a personal privilege for her alone, rarely bestowed and something to treasure.

Although maybe the smile thing was just her imagination, because it definitely wasn't there anymore.

"We can do all that," he said seriously, his enthusiasm tempered and professional in contrast to her own froth of creative energy and vision. "None of that is overambitious or out of step."

"Not even the new pool?"

"You don't necessarily need a new pool."

"But—"

He grinned suddenly. "Don't knock rectangles. Or squares. You can do some pretty clever things with shapes like that if you mix them up a little."

He let himself in through the child-safe gate and dropped to his knees at the pool edge, plunging his arm past the elbow into the water so he could reach the seam between the steps and the side, then running his hand over the smooth, brightly painted concrete and up under the lip of the rim.

"What are you doing?" Daisy asked.

"Checking if it seems structurally sound."

That water wasn't warm! Halfway between the gate and the pool edge, Daisy winced on his behalf, but he seemed untroubled by the water temperature, and when he straightened again, he just ran his other hand down the wet limb to strip most of the water off.

For what felt like far too long, she couldn't look away. It was crazy. The edge of the polo shirt's short sleeve was wet, emphasizing its tight fit against his strong biceps. The sheen of wetness slicked down the hair on his forearm and gave the remnants of his summer tan an extra glow.

He had incredible arms.

Beautiful arms.

What on earth was she doing, thinking that Lee's ex-fiancé had beautiful arms!

"It'll need to be emptied and refinished," he said, forcing her focus back where it belonged. "You might want to clad it in tile. There are some great effects you can achieve with current designs. But we'll get a proper structural check done, obviously, before we start on the work."

"You do pools as well as landscaping?"

"We work with another contractor on that, but it'll be done as part of our overall plan. I'm thinking you might want to put in some solar heating for it, as well." There were goose bumps on the wet arm now, but he was just grinning as he showed them to her.

Wow, the second grin he'd given in the space of a few minutes! On top of that possible smile a little earlier, he was really lightening up! She was the one feeling too serious right now—seriously alarmed about the way her focus kept catching on the powerful maleness of his body... and *liking* it.

"I'm sorry!" She grimaced about the goose bumps on his arm, but the words were a coded warning to herself, as well.

Stop looking, Daisy. Haven't you seen a well-built man before?

"Don't worry," he said. "It's October, I was expecting it. It's not the first time my job has required a bit of cold water."

"So you're just talking about retiling and heating for the pool? Is that enough to bring it up to date?"

"No, those are only details. Let me talk you through this." He began to sketch out his ideas with gestures that took in the whole area. To see it from his viewpoint she had to stand beside him, closer than she really wanted. "Take out this fence and put in one that encloses the playground, as well," he said. "That gets rids of your repeating rectangles."

Another flashback of Michael and those last difficult months at Niche hit her as Tucker spoke—the way Michael would always stand deliberately too close when they went through the dessert menu together, as if to remind her that they'd once been intimate.

Tucker was so different. The opposite. There was a kind of force field in place. Not even the hint of an accidental touch from him. No warmth from his body drifting against her skin.

"Add different levels, raised beds and plantings, seating areas that are like outdoor rooms," he was saying, "so that parents can watch their kids playing and swimming from various vantage points. Create options for sitting in the shade or in the sun. And even though the barbecue area won't be within the fenced enclosure, we'll make it part of the same landscape, carrying through the idea of a variety of seating areas and outdoor rooms, and changing levels."

"It sounds gorgeous," she said. "There's really been nothing for adults anywhere near the playground and pool. Most parents look as if they're doing a penance, minding their kids at the pool. For years it hasn't had as much use as it should."

"What's the room at the end of the building just there?"

"Oh, you mean— That's the laundry room." He was pointing at it, the dullest space at the whole resort, with the possible exception of the sheds tucked away out of sight, where they stored equipment and tools.

"Is there any way that could be moved?"

"Move the room?"

"Change it. Move the laundry facilities somewhere else and revamp that room, extend it, with sliding double-glazed doors on three sides. Slate or tiled flooring. Cedar benches. A hot tub. Make it a spa section that can be open air in the warm weather and enclosed when it's cold."

"That's beyond landscaping, isn't it?"

"You mean, I'm straying outside my brief?"

"No, I'm just stunned, that's all. This is more than I expected from you. Far more."

"You thought I'd be all about azaleas and birch trees?"

"You haven't yet mentioned a single plant."

"Put in a zillion plants without changing the layout and flow of this place, and you'll have spent money for nothing. You have to start with the structure. With the bones."

She shivered, suddenly, as a stray piece of cloud crossed the sun.

The bones.

What was happening in *her* bones this morning? She felt aware and alive in a way that she couldn't put down purely to the fall sunshine or the excitement of the new future for Spruce Bay. Her senses seemed more acute, her mind buzzing, and Tucker dominated all of it. It unsettled her too much. She had to somehow shake it off.

"Shall we look at the lake frontage now?" she said quickly, needing to be on the move again. She hurried to open the pool gate without giving him time to reply.

Chapter Six

Start with the bones.

The words he'd used echoed in Tucker's own head as he followed Daisy along a pine needle-covered path that ran between the cabins and down to the water. He tried to think about the Spruce Bay landscaping contract, the reason he was here...

Yes, she was right, it definitely needed some thinning out of the trees, but not too much, and not everywhere. You didn't want to lose it all to sunny glare for the sake of opening the views...

But it was no good. He had to fight for concentration, because he was feeling something down to the bones, and he wanted it to go away.

Down to the bones.

Bones knew nothing.

But they ached like sore muscles when you had to fight as hard as Tucker was fighting right now.

It's a job, a project, a contract, he coached himself. Just because it's Daisy Cherry, and she's doing to my dumb bones the same thing she did to them ten years ago…

He did *not* give in to transient emotions, no matter how powerful they seemed while he was feeling them. Heaven knew, his marriage certificate ought to be enough of a disincentive, on top of the legacy of his father's affair all those years ago.

The affair was long gone, of course, but the marriage was another matter. Tucker had married Emma for practical, legal reasons, and he'd been incredibly careful to make sure this didn't change.

Fortunately, Emma had been in complete agreement—despite what his mom had claimed yesterday—and now that their divorce was grinding its way through the system, he could look back on the whole thing and think that they'd both been lucky.

Lucky that it had worked as intended, with no chemistry on either side. Lucky it hadn't turned into the kind of mess he hated so much. Lucky that they were both decent people who could keep their eye on the prize.

"One thing I want, and I hope you'll agree to it," he had said to Emma the night they'd made their plans. "No affairs while we're together."

"No affairs?"

"No relationships…flings…involvements, whatever you want to call them, with anyone else on the side."

"Do you really think I'm contemplating anything like that right now?" She'd tensed her thin shoulders and looked over at Max, her seven-year-old son, as he watched TV. He was ill, and it showed. He'd lost his hair to chemotherapy and he was small for his age.

"Of course I don't, but it's something we need to talk about," he'd urged her.

"We've already agreed this is a marriage in name only, for Max's sake."

"And I wanted to cover the other side of the equation."

"Consider it covered, Tucker. I have no intention of getting involved with anyone while Max is so ill. It would be confusing for him, when he knows you and I are going to be married. It would just be wrong!"

"I'm glad you agree. I'm glad I don't have to spell it all out."

"Tucker, you're a decent, honorable man. You put family first. That's one of the things that's making this marriage possible in the first place."

Honorable. A neat little word in Emma's very mixed-up half-English accent.

It hadn't been a word he'd ever thought to attach to himself, but once Emma had used it, he decided that it fit and he was comfortable inside its skin. If honor meant doing unto others as you wanted them to do to you, if it meant taking pride in honesty and fair dealings, if it meant adhering to a code of decency that he couldn't spell out but that might include rules such as, "Don't get a woman pregnant when you're married to someone else and then announce that you're damn well *dying,* Dad!" then, yes, okay, he was honorable and that was good.

He and Emma were both clear on exactly where they stood. Their marriage was going to be a quiet sort of thing, not actively hidden, but not widely announced, either. Known only to those who needed to know it. Just there, in the background, until Emma and Max didn't need it anymore.

Which was about now. The goal had been achieved. Now ten years old, Max had completed his treatment and was in full remission. Emma's citizenship was secured, and whether Max's cancer did or didn't come back, the two of them could legally stay in the only place Max had ever known as home.

It would have been terrible if mother and son had had to leave the country in the middle of Max's illness, to set up a new home in England. Emma was a British citizen, but she hadn't lived there since she was twelve, thanks to her father's roving career. Her parents had retired to the Mediterranean coast in Turkey, so she would have had no family support. Tucker and Emma had filed for their divorce just over two months ago, which meant that it should be final, depending on the workings of the court, in around four weeks.

Just to be totally clear, he did *not* follow passionate impulses, he reminded himself. He was practical and honorable, as Emma had always said, but unfortunately his body didn't seem to have received the memo on either of those things today. It was telling him loud and clear that he and Daisy were meant to be together—for a night or a week or a year or a lifetime, his body was maddeningly nonspecific on that point.

And about the only thing *he* was clear on was that he didn't trust it and didn't want to give in to it and most definitely didn't want to let it show.

Call him cautious, call him damaged, call him anything, he didn't want to turn this flaming, unlooked-for attraction into a huge mistake. Just because a feeling was strong and overwhelming didn't mean it was right to go where it pointed. He'd learned that young, when he'd watched his father's denial of his own mortality turn into such a massive family betrayal.

Tucker and Daisy spent another half hour touring the resort, with him doing his best impression of a block of solid wood, holding his body together, holding his expressions in check, holding his voice to a clipped professional

sort of growl. Back at the Spruce Bay office, he went
through his standard spiel about putting together a package including cost estimate with detailed breakdowns.

This morning, just as he'd been about to leave the office to come here, he'd taken a phone call from a client
postponing a scheduled project roughly the same size as
this one, which had been due to start in fewer than two
weeks. The four-week gap in his usually tight fall calen-
dar now yawned in front of him, demanding to be filled,
but he hadn't said anything to Daisy about it yet.

Now was the obvious time, and the Spruce Bay project was the obvious solution to any potential downtime
for his crew.

And yet he didn't mention it.

"Can I ask, are you getting estimates from any other
companies on this project?" he asked instead.

"I'm not sure." She looked down at the desk and folded
back the creased corner of a page of her notes. "I've done
some research. Yours is the name that always comes up."
She looked across at him, serious and intent. "The Mission Point Hotel, Grantham Gardens, the extensions to
the theme park...*Escapade,* or whatever they're calling
it now."

"We did all those," he confirmed.

"I took a look at them. They were great, really inspir-
ing."

In other words, she'd done her research and the Cherry
family wasn't seriously considering any other company
for the work they wanted. It was a gesture of faith that
he could...*should*...reward with the offer of an imminent
start to the project. Fewer than two weeks. They could
start in fewer than two weeks.

But all the same, he didn't say it.

They were done, for now.

He went through all the right motions, saying he would let her know as soon as the estimate package was ready. She could pick it up from the office, or Jackie could bring it over. He climbed into his vehicle and made what felt like an escape, not simply a departure. He felt as if he was steaming inside his shirt, and it took a twenty-minute journey to the half-finished site he needed to check over before his body got back to normal.

His head took longer.

It took until four that afternoon, when he finally realized that he *had* to call Daisy to tell her about the four-week opening in his schedule or Jackie would be questioning his sanity and his professional judgment.

Jackie, who'd been working with him since he started Reid Landscaping. Jackie, who was the one who'd said to him after Emma had been in tears about her citizenship complications and Max's cancer… Hodgkin's lymphoma, the same thing that had killed Tucker's father… "Why don't you marry her, Tucker? Then she can stay here legally, and Max can continue the treatment with no upheaval and no delay."

He knew very well that he'd have to answer to Jackie if he didn't fill the newly opened hole in their schedule with a solid project.

Back in his office, he picked up the phone and dialed the Spruce Bay number, feeling his heartbeat quicken like a teenager's when he heard the ring at the other end of the line. "Spruce Bay Resort," said a female voice.

"Daisy?"

"No, it's Denise."

Lee's mom. She hadn't said much after the canceled wedding, and that told its own story, because she'd been frothy and talkative with him through the whole engagement, visibly thrilled about her daughter's choice of groom, welcoming him into the family with an eagerness that would have been almost smothering if Lee hadn't kept a healthy sense of humor and balance about it. "I'd better ration your face time with my female parental unit, Tucker, or you won't be able to breathe."

He couldn't breathe now. Denise Cherry was a sweet lady and she terrified him, because he'd already messed things up with one of her daughters, and if there was any risk of him doing it again with a different daughter, the reproach would be more than he could take.

Words backed up in his throat, and before he could speak and give his name, she said brightly, "I'll get her for you, just a moment, please."

He let out a whoosh of thankful breath that she hadn't asked who was calling, or recognized his voice.

"He says there's been an unexpected postponement to another project, which means they can start on Spruce Bay the week after next," Daisy told her mom and dad.

"That's moving very fast," her dad said. He was reacting with an instinctive suspicion about Tucker that made ten years seem like a few months. "That puts them on site at the same time as the crews doing the interior remodeling."

"I told him that, and he says it won't be a problem, they'll make sure they don't block access, or get in each other's way."

"It gives us no time to really think it through. Don't you think it would be better to wait until spring?"

"And it's Tucker Reid we're talking about," her mom added. "If I'd known that just now, when I picked up the phone…! Are you sure this is a good idea, Daisy?"

"You and Mary Jane are both making this too personal, Mom," she answered. "Isn't the goal to limit the length of time Spruce Bay is closed? If we could be up and running again by mid-December, or even sooner, so that we have some occupancy over Christmas and during the winter festivals in February, our cash flow will be a lot healthier. Then we can have the planting done in April, during our usual month of spring shutdown—"

She stopped, hearing that she had run on too long. She'd been gabbling in order to distance the issue of Tucker Reid. Her mom and dad were nodding in dazed agreement.

Her dad said a little helplessly, "You've thought about this more strategically than we have."

"We've all agreed it's time for you two to step back."

"We've been focused too much on the interiors. But you're right, the landscaping is important, and so is the timing."

"It's vital. Tucker has some great ideas. I really don't think we can afford to lose his input just because—" She didn't want to put the reasons into words.

Because of Lee.

Because of *me*.

And that was crazy, since there was no reason that Tucker should be an issue for her.

Her mom and dad nodded again. Her mom sighed. "I'm glad you're here, Daisy. I can't help but make it personal."

"Well, it isn't," Daisy said briskly. "And I'm not having a problem about it."

"Go ahead, then. You said the scheduling window won't be open for long."

"His work is in heavy demand."

Denise sighed again, and Daisy went to call Tucker back. "We want to go ahead, Tucker. We'll take advantage of the time frame that's opened up."

"Great," he said gruffly. "Thanks for making a quick

decision. I couldn't have held that window open for you for very long."

"No problem. It was obvious that we needed to think quickly."

They had a start date locked in before they even had a costing or a plan.

For some reason, it seemed appropriate to be doing this in a backward kind of way, and for it all to be happening very fast. While Mary Jane climbed Mount Kilimanjaro and took pictures of lions and elephants on her phone, Daisy immersed herself completely in paving samples, pool-tile colors, bench options, stonework options, decking options...until even her dreams were filled with it all.

Over the next ten days, she saw Tucker or spoke to him on the phone at least once a day, sometimes twice, and during one memorable four-hour stretch while they went back and forth over the availability and cost of a certain kind of paver for the new pool surround, eleven times.

They faxed each other. They emailed. They texted. They remained utterly professional and almost embarrassingly impersonal through the whole thing, and there was something about it that Daisy seriously didn't trust.

Work on the landscaping began exactly two weeks after she'd first brought up Tucker's name to Mary Jane.

Chapter Seven

Work on the landscaping began with a crash. Or several.

In California, Daisy had been accustomed to getting out of bed in the morning at eight or nine o'clock, after her working day at the restaurant ended late in the evening. With construction crews on site at Spruce Bay at seven in the morning to work on the interiors starting at the beginning of the previous week, she'd reluctantly decided it was best not to still be in her pajamas at seven-thirty.

Last night, though, she'd slept badly, so she fumbled a sleepy hand to turn off the alarm when it sounded at six-thirty, and was still in bed, now, at seven forty-five.

Crash!

Crash, with a background engine rumble. Okay, now she was awake. Confused about what was going on, she scrambled out of bed and went to the window, swiping open the drapes. Nothing problematic visible at first glance. She dragged up the sash and the screen and leaned out because that crashing sound had come from somewhere to the left.

It came again, and she leaned more, blinking in the morning light and stretching to see.

It was some kind of Bobcat or dozer, and it was pushing the old pool fence down so that it crashed onto the concrete that would soon also be disappearing.

She saw Tucker yelling to one of his workers above the noise of the Bobcat, but couldn't hear what he was saying. Then he saw her. He stopped speaking and seemed to freeze for a moment, then gave a slow wave, with no smile on the side. She waved back and called to him, "Everything okay?"

But he couldn't hear her. He shrugged, still unsmiling.

She cupped her hands around her mouth and called louder, "Is everything okay? Do I need to come down?"

He heard this time, and yelled back, "Everything's fine. Come down if you want." Not exactly the most enthusiastic invitation.

She nodded and leaned back into her room, then realized what the outward lean had treated him to. A very personal view down the front of her V-necked pink-and-white-patterned pajama top. Not *that* far. Not really very far at all, she reassured herself. She just hoped he wouldn't think she'd done it on purpose.

But why would I do that? And why would he think it?

For some reason, she didn't want to examine either of these questions too closely. She raced into the shower, stood under hot needles of water and soaped herself for a barely useful length of time, then dived into some clothes, which stuck to her limbs due to her twenty seconds of inadequate toweling.

She was downstairs and outside in about four minutes, tops.

The pool fence was already flattened and in the process of being piled into a skip. A machine had begun plowing up the lawn. Tucker was in consultation with the subcontractor who was extending the restaurant deck and building a set of wide wooden steps all along one side, to improve the flow between the restaurant and the grounds.

"We can order the extra wood today and have it delivered with the original shipment tomorrow, as scheduled," the subcontractor was saying.

"Can you, John?" Tucker looked pleased. "That makes the idea even more attractive."

"The width of the steps would easily accommodate them."

Tucker turned to her. "Daisy, we're talking about having some built-in wooden planter boxes coming down the steps to soften the transition from the deck to the ground."

"Oh, I like that!" She could picture it, and since it was a much more comfortable picture than the one she'd recently had in her head—the view down her pajama top, from Tucker's position—she kept it. "How much extra seating will we have?"

"At least three tables of four. Right, John?" He turned to the other man.

"And I think we'll fill them, once word gets out," Daisy said. "It'll be a gorgeous place to sit. Yes, definitely go for the planter boxes."

"Thanks, bud."

"I'll show you the revised plan when it's done," John told him.

"Send it to my phone, could you?"

"No problem."

"Daisy, let me show you those pavers for the pool surround." Tucker began walking toward one of the trucks and she followed him.

"Oh, they've arrived?" She added quickly, "I'm sorry I slept in this morning, of all days."

"Not important." He sounded gruff and a little reluctant.

She risked a sideways glance, struggling to keep up with his brisk pace. He had his eyes fixed ahead, unreadable as ever, and she was hit suddenly with a flood of awareness and need and frustration that took her breath away.

This was desire.

This was physical.

And it was *sudden*.

He was pulling on her like a magnet, despite every moment of impersonal distance and every closed expression and every instance when he should have smiled at her and didn't.

And she was frustrated about it because she wanted more.

She wanted to touch him. She wanted to look at him, and she gave in to it, because it was just too impossible not to. He really was walking too fast for her, which meant she was treated to a back view—the sight of the jeans that clung to his strong legs and tight male backside, the broad shoulders in their hardworking shirt, the dark hair he'd had cut since last week, so that it skimmed the curved line of his neck and showed the beautiful shape of his head.

"The color is a bit different from the samples I had on hand," he was saying. "It's a different batch. That happens sometimes."

"Is it a problem?"

"I think this tone is better, actually. It's a little lighter and warmer. Since you're going for the darker pool tile, you'll get a nice contrast. But take a look. We can send them back if you're not happy."

They reached the truck and he pulled the top paver off a piled wooden pallet. She couldn't help looking at the way his muscled forearms framed the smooth stone square and it distracted her, until his prompting "So?" reminded her that she had to give a response.

"Can I see it lying flat, by the pool? You have it in shadow, and it looks grayer than I was expecting."

"Sure." He set off back toward the pool and she wondered if he thought she was being difficult, finicky.

He was so polite, so hard to read. She kept expecting something to soften, for him to get a little lighter and more personal in their interactions, drop a joke occasionally or say something about his private life, mention a wife or a girlfriend or a new baby so that she would know he was out of bounds, but if anything, the distance in him had increased through their frequent communications these past ten days.

After a few steps, he turned back on his tracks. "Need more than one, I think." He took three more from the truck. "And I'll grab a couple from this other pallet, the ones with the curve."

"Let me get them, Tucker. You have your arms full already."

"You sure?"

But she'd already darted forward and taken hold of them, suddenly eager to see how they would look.

They were heavier than she'd expected, and she could only carry two with comfort, while Tucker held his four under one arm with no visible effort. Over by the pool, he laid them flat on the cracked concrete, dropping easily to ground level and lining them up with practiced hands. "Here, give me yours." He slid them from her grasp and they came close to touching.

Close, but not quite.

She felt the brush of his shirtsleeve against the sleeve of her top and caught the scent of him, a mix of musk and wood and fresh earth. For a long and helpless moment, she just wanted to close her eyes and breathe, and breathe, and breathe.

"Picture them with the darker tile beneath," he suggested, and it broke the moment just in time.

Or I would have given something away, I know it. Her whole body had begun a slow throb, and the nerve endings in her skin were skittish and fluttering. "You're right," she said not quite steadily. "They're beautiful."

"Are your mom and dad around to take a look?"

"They're in South Carolina this week. They didn't want to get in the way."

"The crew's way?" He gave her a sideways glance that almost had a smile in it. "Or yours?"

It was the most personal thing he'd said to her in days, and it sent arrows of…something—heat? happiness?—darting through her. She laughed before she could stop herself. "Oh, both! Mom would be second-guessing these, worrying about glare. Dad would be trying his darndest to break one, to see whether they're too fragile."

"They're not, and the matte finish should deal with any glare."

"Be thankful they're in South Carolina, or Dad would be asking you about this stuff twenty times a day." She smiled at him in the hopes of coaxing an answering smile back, but nope, nothing happened.

She might have put it down to his having no sense of humor, except that she'd heard him joshing with Jackie and cheerfully teasing another staff member last week while she was in his showroom looking through the Spruce Bay plans. He smiled and laughed with other people often and easily, just not with her.

Let it go, Daisy, she coached herself. You fancy him a little bit...more than a little bit...but he doesn't feel the same about you, so let it go. It's safer that way.

"We'd better put these back," he said after a moment. "You've seen enough?"

"Yes, I'm really happy." She watched him stack the four pavers, and then lay the two with the curved rims on top. "You can't carry all that!"

He shrugged. "It's fine."

And it seemed to be. He was strong, adept, easy about the load, and when they got back to the truck, he slid them onto the pallet with just the right gentle shove so that they stacked neatly but didn't scrape. She wondered if his hands and body were that good...that experienced and easy...in other areas.

Let it go, Daisy. Do you want *an attraction to someone this distant and prickly?*

Someone who used to be engaged to Lee.

"I have things to do in the office," she said abruptly, needing to get out of his aura, away from the heat she could almost feel, and that he clearly didn't want.

Boring things to do, unfortunately.

He seemed to read her reluctance. "Yeah, I know, I hate when I have to sit looking at screens for hours at a stretch."

"Why does every career seem to require that now? Even as a dessert chef, I was online, researching suppliers and food trends."

"Prison of our own making. Doing plans and designs on a computer is way easier than on paper."

They went in different directions, and Daisy was shocked at the level of tickle and thrill inside her just because of that tiny bit of sharing about sitting in front of screens.

In the family kitchen, she fixed herself coffee and

grape jelly on toast for breakfast and took them across to the resort office, to ease into the task of messing around with the numbers. Offer a white Christmas special deal maybe? Would the increased occupancy offset the lower room rates?

She surprised herself by getting completely immersed in the work. The coffee and toast were long gone, and in another half hour, she would have several beautifully laid-out sets of figures to show Mary Jane next week when she arrived back from her trip—and Mom and Dad, also, if they insisted on seeing them.

Now if she just bolded some of these numbers, the whole thing would be even clearer to see at a glance...

She heard footsteps coming onto the porch, and saw Tucker's outline looming through the window. Scraping her hair behind her ears, she did a quick save on the computer and then there he was. "Do you want me?" she asked brightly.

A question that could have been phrased better, Daisy Cherry, under the circumstances.

He gave a short nod and launched into a long and complex explanation about subsiding earth on the slope of ground heading down to the lake where they were putting in stone steps and compacted gravel paths. "It's going to cost," was the rather blunt and distant warning he finished with.

"I'd better come look for myself, right?"

"Sorry to interrupt." As gruff as ever.

"No, it's good that I'm on site for this kind of thing."

They walked side by side across what used to be the lawn and was now a flat mass of dirt littered with equipment and piles of supplies. In two of the cabins, she could hear the contractors at work on the remodeled bathrooms—men she'd been consulting with for days, offering coffee to occasionally, sharing a joke with once or twice.

Just men.

But this was Tucker beside her, and he was different. Something told her this in a way she couldn't ignore or talk herself out of. In the silence between them, she felt his pull growing, showing itself in her body's mounting heat, her breathing's fraying edge, just her whole awareness.

It was a stupid word, *awareness,* but it fit. She was *aware* in a way that felt too intense. She could sense the way his body filled the space beside her, the way it moved. She wanted to strain for the sound of his breathing, look across to see the rhythm of his walk.

With increasing need, she wanted some kind of response from him. She wanted Tucker to notice her as a woman, to find her attractive. She wanted to get through to him on that elemental male-and-female level. It was starting to kill her a little bit inside that he seemed so oblivious and distant, with a wall in place that she couldn't interpret no matter how much she tried.

Did he not like her as a person? Did he have rules about clients? Was it still because of Lee and the canceled wedding ten years ago? Was Mary Jane right, and he just wasn't an especially nice person? Cold, or something?

She felt like a teenager, or like the twenty-one-year-old she'd been back when they'd known each other before, too new at this adult stuff to get it right.

Which was crazy, because she was thirty-one now.

So what did a woman on the wrong side of the big three-oh do in a situation like this?

Think about it, Daisy, you know this…or you should. *She lets him know.*

She lets her eyes say it, lets her hip brush a little too close. Pulls back if he doesn't give her anything in return.

She could let it go *then,* not now, when she had no real indication of what his response might be. Her head began to spin with hope and possibilities and fear. It was scary to think of putting herself on the line like that, scary to let herself in for the whole roller-coaster ride, but she hated holding back in life. How could you be a miser about your own feelings?

They'd reached the section of slope that Tucker wanted to show her. It was quiet out here. The noise and activity of the work on the resort was all happening elsewhere. You could still hear the faint sound of a tile cutter on a far cabin porch, and a Bobcat moving earth near the pool, but those were background sounds, less dominant than the sound of water lapping the hulls on the boats docked on the lake just below them, or the rustle of falling leaves stripped loose by a rising breeze.

"The plan calls for a series of steps and landings down here," Tucker said. "But when I look at the slope, it's not stable enough. The landing will subside at this point."

"And look ugly?"

"That, and eventually it'll be unsafe."

"So what are our choices?"

"We could switch to wooden steps, which can be anchored in place by wooden supports driven well into the ground. Or we can put in better structural work to stabilize the slope, and stick to what we decided before—the compacted gravel and the stone."

"Hmm." He was distracting her, and the little agenda of carefully letting him know that she fancied him was distracting her more. Should she do it?

She stepped back just so she could watch him better. He'd done that crouch thing again, the way he had by the pool, getting down low to examine the seam of sandier soil that was part of the problem he'd found. She liked the way he moved, sure and economical and strong, focused and—

"Do you want the cost comparison before you make a decision?" he prompted, sharply putting her focus back to where it should have been.

"Oh, um… Yes. I think so."

"I should have it for you tomorrow, in that case. Is that soon enough?"

"It's great, Tucker." She stepped forward and touched his forearm as a way of saying thanks…and a way of testing him.

He looked down at the unexpected contact, his skin warm even through the sleeve of his work shirt. Daisy looked down at it, too. There was plenty of time because time had stopped completely. They'd both frozen in place, locked together by the simple act of her placing a palm on the muscle of his lower arm and leaving it there.

Her heart was beating. The moment seemed ridiculously important, as if she would live or die by the way he reacted, whether he threw her off, ignored her touch or pulled her closer. Which would it be?

This is a question, Tucker, and I'm waiting for your answer. This is me, laying myself on the line and telling you what I want, waiting to see if you want it, too. You haven't showed me much, but I just have this feeling…

Would he kiss her? Reach a hard hand to the back of her neck and draw her in so that they pressed together length to length? Let out a sigh of exultant relief because he'd been feeling this, too, and at last one of them had dared to make a move?

Or would he pretend it wasn't happening, and say something inane and practical about treated timber or cement-truck access?

No.

None of the above.

They were both still looking down at the join between them, the shared warmth of hand and arm, the closeness, the message. Seconds had passed. Or maybe not, because time really did not seem to be functioning the way it usually did.

But then, finally, he picked up her hand. Just *picked it up* the way he might have picked up a dry leaf that had settled there, or, no, a beetle—a pretty one that he didn't want to hurt, but that couldn't be permitted to stay where it was, because it didn't belong there. Picked it up and gave it back to her.

Here is your hand, Daisy. It accidentally fell onto my arm and I'm carefully lifting it off so it doesn't get hurt, but I don't want it there. Okay?

She began to burn inside as she stepped clumsily back, and she knew that her cheeks were burning, too, betraying her even more than her own actions had done. Beyond that one gesture of rejection, Tucker hadn't moved, hadn't said a word, hadn't changed the neutral expression on his face, and yet she was in no doubt about what had just happened.

She'd acted and he'd reacted. She'd asked and he'd answered. There didn't need to be anything further.

Message received, Tucker.

Message received loud and clear.

Her insides lurched and sank in disappointment.

Chapter Eight

Tucker was running late, driving back from Vermont. He'd had a final site visit with a client this morning for a project he'd done in the Burlington area and it had gone overtime. He'd wanted to be on site at Spruce Bay for the concrete pour, but since traffic through Queensbury wasn't cooperating, he accepted that the concrete pour was happening without him, and sent a phone message to the guys to tell them he wouldn't be there.

He arrived at around three to find the cement truck gone, the concrete already partially smoothed around the pool and his new employee, Kyle, mucking around while seasoned Reid Landscaping site manager Brad growled at him to take himself seriously and get on with the job.

They were going to have problems with Kyle.

Tucker strode closer, ready to intervene. The new guy was around twenty-two years old, skinny but strong, cheerful but vague, well-intentioned but clueless. Right now, he teetered on the edge of the fresh pour, asking nineteen-year-old Scott, "Haven't you always wanted to do it? Step in this stuff?" He had Scott by the arm, threatening to knock him off balance and into the wet cement.

"Quit it, Kyle," Scott said. He could clearly tell that Brad wasn't in the mood for this, and both he and Brad had seen Tucker's approach.

Kyle hadn't, apparently. He teetered more, beginning to look as if he was losing control. Looking *wrong*, somehow. His hands had begun to jerk. He tilted off axis as if his brain couldn't tell which way was up. Was the idiot still just messing around?

Scott shook off the other guy's grip, not wanting to spoil his own record of good work by association with this character. Kyle staggered backward into the fresh cement, leaving deep, dragging tracks, then he swiveled crookedly and pitched and staggered in the opposite direction, into the pool they'd drained a few days ago ready for the retiling, leaving just an inch or two of murky water still needing to be pumped out.

He landed with a crack of bone on concrete, which Tucker heard clearly, even though he was still a good fifteen yards away. He quickened his approach and yelled, "Sheesh…jeez! Is he okay, Brad?"

"Not moving." The site manager vaulted down into the pool, while Scott swore repeatedly and seemed fiercely determined to get back to work, as if he thought he'd be in trouble if he didn't.

"I'm calling 911." Tucker reached for the phone that should have been in his pocket, then remembered he'd texted Brad from the side of the road in Queensbury and flung the phone onto the passenger seat, intending—but then forgetting—to grab it again when he got out of the car. "Don't move him. I don't know what that cracking sound was, but if he has neck or spinal injuries…"

"That part I do remember," Brad said.

Brad and Scott didn't carry their phones when they were doing things like pouring concrete, Tucker knew. "I'll call from the office." He picked his way back past the half-spread piles of wet gray slop, thinking that if it wasn't finished soon it would start to set in place, and it would be a pain in the butt to remove. Hell, he knew it was wrong to feel angry with Kyle over the work disruption when the guy was hurt, but he felt it anyhow.

As he approached the office, Daisy came out to meet him. She'd seen that something was wrong. "What is it?"

She folded her arms across her front in an unconsciously defensive gesture Tucker was growing accustomed to by now. He was responsible for it, he guessed. She wore jeans and a thin, figure-hugging light blue sweater with a line of intricate gold embroidery around the neckline, and when she did that thing with her arms it had the effect of pushing her neat, rounded breasts up. The sweater showed every change in contour.

Shoot, he couldn't look…must not look. He told her, "Kyle fell in the pool and he's out cold."

"What did he hit? Just his head?"

"Don't know."

She whirled around and hurried back onto the porch and through the door, and had the phone in her hand by the time he reached her. He almost went to grab it from her, but she seemed cool and clear as she spoke to the dispatcher. "We have a man injured on a work site, and he's unconscious. We need an ambulance."

A week had gone by since that moment out by the lake when she'd put her hand on his arm, and he'd thought about it countless times since. It had been so clear what she was asking, and what she wanted.

Hell, he thought again.

He'd turned into a block of stone in that moment, trying to control what he gave back in reply. Her aura had surrounded him like honey or light or magic. He could so, so easily have leaned into it, leaned down, brushed his forehead against hers, looked for her mouth, found the sweet fruit of her lips and closed the space between their bodies until they were locked together, thigh to thigh, chest to soft breasts, mouth to mouth, sigh to sigh.

He'd lived all those actions, and more, in anticipation and need, and then he'd taken a grip and hadn't done it, not any of it. He'd just taken her hand away, his teeth hurting from clenching them so hard, and had watched her step awkwardly back with pink color flaming in her cheeks, almost matching the bright cherry-pink top she'd been wearing that day.

He had no doubt that she was clear on what he was telling her.

Thanks, but no thanks.

It had been so damned hard!

Yeah, and take the double meaning in that sentence if you want.

Since then, they'd avoided each other. Or rather, avoided being alone with each other. When they needed to consult over the project, they exchanged text messages and arranged meetings in the thick of the work, where the presence of Brad or Scott or Kyle could ease the atmosphere.

And now Kyle was lying unconscious at the bottom of the almost-empty pool, while Daisy was giving the address and location of the resort as she leaned her pert, peachy butt on the edge of a computer desk littered with various brochures, a calculator and pages of scribbled notes.

Her blond hair was somewhat untidy today, and she had a tiny smear of dark blue ink on her baby-soft cheek and another on her fingers, and Tucker still wanted her so badly with every cell in his body that it hurt to be in the same space.

Hurt, so he left, seeking the air of a cold, cloudy afternoon that threatened the fresh concrete pour as much as the effect of Kyle's staggering footsteps. There'd been no rain in the forecast, but if it showed up anyhow…

Daisy came out again. "They're on their way."

"Could you grab some blankets? He'll be losing body heat."

"Yes, you're right. I'm sorry, I should have thought of that myself. But I'm—" She slapped the side of her head lightly with the heel of her hand, with her mouth turned in an upside-down smile, and didn't finish the sentence.

"Don't worry about it," he answered, voice all gruff and caught in his throat, because he knew her apology was about the moment by the lake as much as it was about the blankets. She thought it was her fault out there, that she'd got it wrong.

No, you didn't, Daisy. You got it totally right. More right than you could possibly know. There are other reasons, that's all. Messy reasons getting in the way.

She went to the storeroom that opened from the back office and returned a few moments later with a folded pile of blankets tucked into the crook of one arm.

"I don't think he blacked out because he fell in the pool," Tucker told her. The realization caught up with him, finally, although it had been lurking since he'd watched the way Kyle's body was moving, and the stagger of his feet in the wet cement. "I think he fell in the pool because he was blacking out. He was messing around, and then he went off balance... His hands were jerking. I think he was having some kind of seizure or fainting spell."

"Will that make a difference to how they treat him? Should we call the dispatcher back?"

"No, I don't think we need to do that, but we should tell the paramedics when they get here. I'm going to call Jackie in the office in a minute, and get the contact details listed for his next of kin."

"This is terrible." She frowned and dragged her free hand through her hair. It was like messy straw, the fine, fluffy strands sticking out every which way so that his fingers itched to smooth it back from her forehead and behind her ear. "I wasn't too impressed with him, Tucker. I'd thought about having a word with you on the subject. You haven't been on site so much this past week." The words faltered for a moment, as if, once again, she was remembering what had happened a week ago. Was this *why* he hadn't been on site? she was wondering. Was it because he was too embarrassed?

He hated this, ached to tell her that, yes, of course he damn well wanted her! Of course she hadn't been wrong about that! He'd been on fire for her, practically shaking with the effort of overcoming it. But what could he say? How could he say it?

I don't trust this stuff because my dad chose to deal with cancer by leaving a good marriage in the dust, leaving his whole family in the dust, and even if I did trust it, I've promised my wife that I won't get involved with anyone else until our divorce is through. Oh, and in case you're forgetting, I used to be engaged to your sister.

It was the kind of emotional triple-play that could bring consequences—mess and anger and reproach—that he shuddered to contemplate.

Best let it alone, let her think it was a rejection. There was a level of safety in that.

"Brad is competent to manage everything I've left him with," he said. "And I agree with you about Kyle. Brad has spoken to me about him, also."

"I've been hoping he'd quit. Now I feel as if I've ill-wished him."

"No such thing," he told her bluntly.

"You think?"

"I know."

It was part of the long list of things he didn't believe in, because if ill-wishing worked, then Andrea Lewers would be covered in boils like volcanoes and would spit toads every time she talked like some character in a fairy tale, since his mom had been ill-wishing her relentlessly for years.

"Thanks for the reassurance," Daisy said neutrally.

"You're welcome." Then he blurted out her name before he could stop himself. "Daisy…"

"Hmm?" Her eyes were narrowed and she looked tense and he hated it.

"Look, this past week, after we—"

"Tucker," she cut in, more tense than ever, "if you're talking about…out by the lake…can I apologize for that? It was inappropriate. I know that now. And I hoped I'd signaled clearly enough that you wouldn't be subject to a repetition."

"You did. I didn't mean to—" He swore under his breath, wondering what in hell had made him open his mouth. "There was no need for me to bring it up. My turn to apologize."

"Yes, well…" She gave a tight little nod. "We should just let it go."

The tension between them flickered and shifted. There

was no place for it now. They both headed for the pool, Daisy marching ahead with those blankets flopping in her arms.

"He's still not coming round," Brad said when they were close enough to see over the rim. Brad had stayed at Kyle's side, while Scott had flung their jackets down there to cover him with. He seemed to have given up on the idea of continuing work on his own, and was just standing by the edge of the pool.

"Use these," Daisy said, tossing the blankets down. "Let me stay with him until the ambulance gets here. This has happened on our site and I want to take responsibility." She climbed down the dry, blue-painted steps of the pool, and went to kneel beside the unconscious man, ignoring the mucky water that quickly soaked the knees of her jeans. Carefully, she removed the two jackets and spread the blankets instead.

Brad stood up. "Boss?" Tucker wasn't sure what to do, or how to feel. There was an uneasiness in all of them, stemming from the fact that none of them had liked Kyle all that much, but now he was badly hurt and no one would have wanted that.

Looking down at the scene in the pool, Tucker felt a rush of weird relief, seeing Daisy's blond head bent over the injured worker.

"We have this under control," he said. "Daisy's here, the ambulance is coming, he's fully covered by our insurance and I'm about to call Jackie to find out who we need to contact about what's happened. I want you and Scott to get back to work, Brad, okay? There's nothing more we can do for Kyle right now. Let's not add a ruined pour and piles of hardened concrete to this disaster of an afternoon."

A subdued and smaller work crew resumed the task of

smoothing cement, leaving one section of it open to create a safe passage to the pool for the paramedics, while Tucker turned his back on them to speak to Jackie about Kyle's emergency-contact details. He'd listed his mom, but when Tucker tried to call, her phone was switched off.

The ambulance arrived ten minutes later.

"I'm going to follow along," Daisy said after they'd put Kyle in a neck collar, slid a spinal board beneath him, brought him with some difficulty up from the pool and loaded him into the back of the vehicle.

She'd climbed out of the pool, her pretty features all tight. Tucker realized how rare it was for her to look that way. Normally her face was so open and alive, eager and curious and involved. Seeing her like this gave him a powerful need to take action, but he knew he had to let it go. It wasn't his role.

"Did you get ahold of anyone?" she asked, seeing that he still had his phone in his hand.

"Left a message on his mom's phone."

"Give me her number. I'll keep trying her from the hospital." She took out her own phone and stood there with her head bent a little as she input the number, her hand shielding the screen from the light.

"Keep me posted," he told her. "I want to come in and see him…can't imagine they'll send him home today, he's been out cold for a while now."

"I kept hoping for him to groan or move, but he hasn't. I hope we have better news when we get on to his mom."

"Talk soon," he promised, and reached out to squeeze her shoulder before he could stop himself. The rounded muscle there felt slight but firm, strengthened by the physical work required in a big professional kitchen. His thumb slid over the shoulder seam of her blue sweater. The office where she'd been working all morning was warm, and all she wore beneath it was a bra, but out here it was chillier and she looked cold after sitting on the chilly concrete of the pool, at Kyle's side.

He wanted to pull her against him and warm her with his own body heat, feel the press of those sweet, pert breasts, smooth down her mussed-up hair. His thumb slipped again—and okay, it was deliberate—down toward her collarbone.

She looked at him, eyes narrowed, not warning him off but confused, asking a question. *So now you're touching me? Now you're the one invading my space?*

Damn! Damn! Damn!

He let her go, dropped his hand to his side and clenched it into a fist.

"It's almost four," she said. "I'm not going to be back by the time you stop for the day, so could you lock the office? Or ask Tony to, if his crew's still here?" She kept it open for the work crews anytime she wasn't around, in case they needed the fax machine or the refrigerator.

"Sure," he said.

"Thanks."

Within a minute or two, she'd gone, speeding up the driveway in her little red car, leaving him frustrated and cursing himself and still angry at Kyle.

Chapter Nine

"What shall I tell his mother, assuming I can reach her?" Daisy asked one of the nurses at the desk.

The emergency room was quiet. She'd been here over an hour but hadn't been able to find out much. She'd tried Kyle's mother's phone three more times, leaving increasingly urgent messages, but there had still been no response. It was almost six in the evening now.

"He's in a stable condition, and we're waiting on tests," the nurse answered. "I'm sorry, I can't tell you any more than that since you're not next of kin. We would like someone here, if that's possible. You don't have any other contacts for him?"

"No, we don't."

"No one that his workmates know of? People don't always think carefully when they fill in those forms at work. He could have a girlfriend or a roommate, someone else whom he would want to be here."

"He hasn't been working for Reid Landscaping very long, apparently. I'm not sure how much they'll know about his personal circumstances. But you're right. Let me make another call." She went to phone Tucker outside, where daylight had ebbed and the clouds had lowered but the dry weather still held.

"I'll ask Brad and Scott, see if they know who he might want," he said when she'd explained the issue.

"How is the concrete?"

"It's done. It's good. We're about ready to leave, and Tony's crew headed off over an hour ago. They've closed everything up. Just hang on a second." Daisy heard the muffled sound of his voice questioning Kyle's workmates, and then he came back on the line. "He has a girlfriend, Scott says. Her number should be in his phone. That's still in our truck. I'm about to head to the hospital, so I'll bring it and we can hand it over to the staff."

"Okay, yes, that makes sense."

"You'll still be there?"

"I really don't want to leave until Kyle has somebody here."

"We can talk about that when I get there. It's my responsibility more than yours. Reid Landscaping is my company."

"It's my pool, and Spruce Bay is my family's resort. I'll try his mom again."

"Really hope you can reach her."

"Me, too."

"See you in a bit."

That was, what, five words? Five words that echoed in Daisy's head, and that she wanted to treasure. Casual words. She liked that. "See you in a bit" was something you said to people you felt comfortable with, and good about. She liked the idea that maybe Tucker felt good about her, even if he did keep her at a scrupulous distance.

She keyed in Kyle's mother's number yet again, expecting the message service, but this time, finally, someone picked up, at which point Daisy realized she had no idea how to address the person she was talking to. She didn't know the woman's name.

"Is this Kyle's mother?"

"Yes, who is this?" The voice sounded scratchy and distracted.

It was an awkward conversation, and the other woman seemed slow to grasp what had happened. "You mean he's in the hospital right now?"

"Yes."

"So can I speak to him?"

"No, I'm afraid he's still unconscious."

"You want me to come? Are you one of the nurses?"

"No, I'm... He was working on site at a project Reid Landscaping is doing, and I'm—"

But the woman didn't seem interested in the clarification. "I guess I'll come. I'll call a cab, or something."

"If you need—" But Kyle's mother had disconnected the call before Daisy could offer to pick her up, and she was left with no idea of when to expect her arrival.

Tucker should be here soon, she reminded herself.

But he didn't come, and close to another hour passed, which meant it was after seven, and the nurses still had nothing to tell her about Kyle's condition. She sat in the waiting area, perched on the edge of a plastic seat, watching the automatic doors at the entrance swishing open and shut whenever someone went in or out.

Then finally...

"Are you the lady who called me?" The woman was scrappily dressed and poorly groomed. She apologized for both. "I was taking a nap." *Passed out,* Daisy corrected mentally. Kyle's mom reeked of stale alcohol and still sounded slightly slurred. "I'd only just woken up when you called."

"We'll find someone on staff." She stood and put an awkward arm around the woman's shoulders, feeling a surge of sympathy despite the questionable beginning. This was a mother with an injured son. "They'll be able to tell you much more about how Kyle is doing. All they've told me is that he's stable."

But the mom—Daisy still hadn't discovered her name—had her focus fixed elsewhere, in an angry stare. "What the freakin' jeesh is that hellcat doing here?"

The automatic doors had swished open again. Daisy's heart jumped when she saw Tucker, but it was the pretty young woman beside him who had Kyle's mother's attention. "She has no right to be here! None!"

Maybe not, Daisy had no idea about that, but she could see that the girl had been crying, and she still looked agitated and upset, while Kyle's mom still didn't seem to have registered that her son's condition might be serious. She stormed forward and repeated the words to the girl's face. "You have no right to be here."

"He's unconscious, Annette," the pretty brunette said tiredly. "Can we put the rest of it on hold for now?"

"On hold? What do you mean, on hold?"

"Can we maybe forget that we can't stand each other, and remember that we both care about him, or something? Is that too hard?"

"I don't need to hear this. You think you are just so perfect, that you're *better* than me. You think you can tell me how to behave? That is a joke! You're stealing my son away from me—"

An ambulance pulled into the bay outside, lights still

flashing, and there was a commotion as staff hurried to meet the paramedics who climbed out.

"I'm not stealing him. You *push* him away. You *drive* him away. Is it any wonder he has problems?"

A child in the waiting room began to cry loudly. He looked to be around two years old, with his arm in a make-shift sling, and his parents couldn't manage to comfort him. Meanwhile, another set of parents huddled together, whispering fiercely at each other.

"Problems?" Kyle's mother screeched. "Oh, he has *problems?* And those are down to me? Do you have any idea how much grief he's given me? And his father is no help. Seven years of child support he never paid. And you're telling me *he* has problems."

A doctor appeared, and three people went toward him with fear in their faces.

"Your drinking, of course, has nothing to do with any of it," Kyle's girlfriend said in an angry mutter. It was hard to tell if she meant it to be overheard or not, but overheard it was.

"Do you hear how she's talking to me?" Annette turned to Daisy, cheeks aflame with indignation, grabbing her arm as if they were best friends and she could count on Daisy's support.

But Daisy hardly heard her, because all her focus was on Tucker. He had gone progressively paler as the argument progressed and the tension in the waiting area heightened. Now there was no color in his face at all. His jaw was so tightly clenched that she could see the knots of muscle on either side. His eyes were narrowed and he held his body as stiff as a board. The tension in him crackled almost audibly, although Kyle's mother and girlfriend were both too caught up in their own problems to notice.

"This is pointless. I'm not doing this now. I'm just

not," the girlfriend muttered again, half under her breath. "I'm going to find out if we can see him. *He* is the important thing right now, not this stupid, possessive—" She stopped, took control of herself and turned to Tucker. "Thanks so much for bringing me. I was shaking so much when you told me, I don't think I would have been safe to drive."

"You're welcome, Bec." He shook off a little of his visible torment, took her hands between his and squeezed them. "If there's anything I can do, you call, okay?" Daisy could see his struggle to speak calmly. "You have my number. It was a workplace accident, so we'll be covered for that. Mrs. Schramm, or either of you... If you need help with insurance paperwork, or anything else at all, don't hesitate to ask."

Kyle's mother glowered at him, seeming not to know who he was, but prepared to be angry that he was being so civil to the girlfriend she couldn't stand.

Meanwhile, Bec nodded in reply, lifting her chin as if to take a firmer grip on herself. "Thanks. I will. You've been great." Daisy couldn't help admiring her strength and caring, especially in the face of Kyle's mother's attitude. She stepped back, and both women began to walk toward the main desk, Bec leading the way and Mrs. Schramm apparently following only to ensure that she wasn't outmaneuvered in some nasty game that Bec very clearly didn't want to play.

Daisy and Tucker were left standing together, and she could see that all he wanted was to cut and run. He looked as if he was ill, or in pain, or about to lose it—his head, or his lunch.

"I'm sorry I took so long to get here," he said with difficulty. "When I reached Rebecca...Bec...on the phone, she was so upset I ended up going over to their apartment and picking her up. It took a while, and I didn't manage to call you."

"It's fine. I'm glad she's here. The mother…"

"…looks like a problem," Tucker agreed. They looked over at the main desk, where the two women were still visibly bristling at each other while a nurse spoke to them. The fiercely whispering couple a few yards away were getting louder.

"We have to tell the doctor," Daisy heard the woman say.

"No, it's not important," the man replied. "You're totally overreacting, as usual."

Tucker took in a breath, trying to disguise its unsteadiness, and Daisy said quickly, "Let's get out of here."

"Yes." He was already on his way to the door.

"Are you okay?" She followed him, wondering if he was phobic about blood or needles, something that would make sense of his scary level of stress.

"Fine. I'm fine."

"You're not." *Don't yell at him, Daisy.* She lowered her voice, but it was just as intense. "You're really *not*, Tucker." Her feelings for him flared and burned, and she felt so powerless she almost couldn't breathe.

"Sorry. I will be. In a minute." He went for the automatic door on a lunge, barely giving it time to open, and as soon as he was through he began to stride along the concrete sidewalk that ran along the front of the hospital building, and she had to hurry to keep up.

"Don't apologize," she told him. "Can we sit, or something? Catch our breath? That wasn't much fun."

"No, it wasn't."

There was a bench seat ten yards farther on, with a planting of ornamental grasses around it, and Daisy didn't wait for his agreement, she just sat down. He came to a reluctant halt a few strides beyond the bench, wheeled back and joined her, slumping onto the seat as if the effort of holding himself together had left him with energy drained and no breath. They sat in silence for a good minute, while Tucker gave off a brooding aura that told Daisy there was more going on here than she knew. Her heart ached for him.

"That little scene back there seemed to hit you pretty hard," she finally ventured.

"Yeah, sorry." He lifted a hand that might not have been quite steady, and massaged his temples with a thumb and forefinger. Watching tied her in knots.

"Not asking for an apology, Tucker, just wondering if you want to talk about it."

"It's nothing. Memories, that's all." He thought for a moment. "*Flashbacks* might be a better word."

"Memories aren't nothing. Flashbacks even more so."

"I guess not." He fell into another difficult silence, and once more she burned so much to touch him that she didn't know what to do with herself.

"You don't like hospital waiting rooms," she suggested. It sounded so thin, so inadequate.

"No." For a moment, it seemed as if this one syllable was all he had in him, but then he took a breath and said, "Arguments in hospital waiting rooms are worse."

"Had a few of those?" Her voice came out scratchy with uncertainty about the way she was pushing him.

"Been there for them. Tried to hose them down. Watching Kyle's mom and Bec brought it all back." More silence, then, "Sorry, it's not that I don't want to talk about this. Something's telling me I probably should."

"Like the fact that you looked as if you might pass out from stress back there?"

"Yeah, that. I...hadn't expected it. It just hit me like a

train. As if I was back in the same situation, the same…
yeah." He shook his head, eyes closed, as if still fighting
to shake something off. "I don't know, it just feels—" He
stopped again, and made an explosive sound of frustration. "Hell, what am I doing?"

"It's okay," she said inadequately. "I'm listening,
Tucker."

"I know. Doesn't mean I can do this."

"No, I guess not." She realized out loud, "Maybe I'm
not the right person…"

"No, you are. You are the right person." He said it almost absentmindedly, as if his focus was still far more
on the memories, but the words sent a golden shaft of
happiness through her—a crazy, *stupid* golden shaft of
happiness.

A stupid, idiotic golden shaft of happiness that completely robbed her of words, because it was like a bubble,
filling and blocking her lungs.

You are the right person.

So simple and matter-of-fact. You are the right person.
The sun rises in the east. The sky is blue.

Shafts, bubbles… *Daisy, this is just wrong. It makes
no sense.*

But it's happening anyhow.

"My dad got cancer," he said abruptly. "When I was
thirteen. Or I guess he got it before that, but I was thirteen when he told us."

"He didn't tell you right away?"

"Nope. He was behaving strangely. I could tell Mom
was worried. I found her crying a couple times. He kept
coming home late. Or he'd say he was at the office, only
when Mom called the office, he wasn't. And then when
he told us about the diagnosis—it was caught pretty late,
he should have gone to the doctor way sooner about his

symptoms, the prognosis was never great—I had this weird relief in the whole mix. *This* is why he's been lying to us about working late, he's been at the doctor's. Now that he's told us, he and Mom can deal with it together, and he'll get cured, and things will be normal again. I can go back to being a normal kid, in a happy, normal family."

"Only, that didn't happen."

"That didn't happen, and the lying didn't stop with the cancer out in the open. He was having an affair. He'd started the affair because of the cancer, he said. He always blamed the cancer for it, like that meant it was okay, understandable and normal and right. Like a man gets cancer, and anything he does after that is totally acceptable, no matter how selfish or hurtful it is."

He stopped again, broke off a spear of ornamental grass and began shredding it methodically into long, skinny strips with fingers that seemed to know exactly what they were doing even when the task made no sense.

"Was that what the arguments in hospital waiting rooms were about? The affair?"

"Yeah…no. Kind of. They weren't arguments between Mom and Dad, they were arguments between Mom and Andrea. He didn't stop seeing her. In fact, he saw her more, once their relationship was out in the open. He pretty much divided his time. I'd say fifty-fifty. Mom would say we got thirty percent, and Andrea seventy. Andrea was pregnant, she had a little boy."

"Oh, Tucker!"

"We spent the last three years of Dad's life dealing with his illness and this other family he felt entitled to have, and who we were just supposed to accept, the way you're supposed to accept the person you love going bald from chemo. And, you know, of course you accept the chemo, but is having another family really in that same category?"

He didn't need her answer, but she gave it anyhow. "No, it's not."

He went on without a pause, "Dad always acted as if it was totally his decision. Two families. Nonnegotiable. No one else had the right to set boundaries or have their feelings consulted. Andrea wanted to be at his bedside, and she wanted her son...their son...to be with his dad, and Mom felt for the kid...Jonah, my half brother...because it wasn't his fault, but that meant these ongoing encounters with Andrea, who resented us as much as we resented her, and all these..." He trailed off, tightened his jaw.

"All these arguments in hospital rooms?"

"Yeah."

He sketched it out in more detail, as if he couldn't dam up the memories now that he'd let them loose. He talked about fights over who got to consult with the doctors, about his father's attempts to intervene and hose things down. "And it was always about him. And I felt so angry. And so guilty. He had cancer. It *was* about him. But that seemed to come with such a limitless sense of entitlement on his part."

He talked about his mom taking Jonah for a milkshake one day so that Dad and Andrea could have some time alone, after Dad had asked for it, and then Tucker's own discovery later that his mom had gone to Andrea's place that same night and punctured all her car tires.

"And I understood...hell, I would have grabbed a pocket knife and helped her...because it was hitting me that way, too. Trying so hard to do the right things, keep my brother and sister from getting hurt, but gripped by such anger... I had to go see Andrea and beg her not to call the police about the tires. She knew Mom was the culprit. And Dad just kept saying, 'For my sake.' We all had to behave perfectly for his sake, his two families, because he had cancer, so he got to do and feel whatever he liked."

"Oh, Tucker…" There was simply nothing else to say.

"And when Lee was in the hospital after her accident, I was focused on her, not on my own stuff. Today, with all that hostility between Bec and Mrs. Schramm, it brought it all back. But I really, seriously was not expecting it. I mean, hell, it's a long time ago, now, eighteen years and more, but it took me right back to that period when I suddenly had to grow up and didn't want to. I really wasn't expecting that level of intensity in the way I reacted. I'm really sorry."

"Tucker, don't apologize! How is it your fault?"

"Putting you through it. Spilling it all out like that."

"I wanted to hear it. Lee never told us any of this."

There was a moment's pause before he answered, then he said quietly and simply, "Lee didn't know." He glanced at her and their eyes met for a moment, like a dazzle of sunlight breaking between trees, but then he looked back down at his restless fingers, shredding another long strand of drying grass.

"Oh," Daisy said, and that look between them froze in her awareness as if it was still happening. Blazing and short-lived and utterly confusing in its power.

"I just…it just never felt right to tell her," he said, low and husky. "Especially after her accident."

"About the arguments?"

"About any of it. Andrea, Jonah. She knew my parents had had a few problems before Dad died. I just…" He shrugged. "I guess it was still too fresh. I was twenty-four, but still I didn't have the words. Or Lee and I didn't have that kind of relationship or something. We were all about getting out there and skiing or hiking or rock climbing, not about talking, not about digging through the past, looking for damage. We just didn't...share that kind of stuff."

"Right...okay."

"Maybe that should have told us something. Maybe the reason we never seemed to have any peace and quiet between us wasn't because of the accident or the wedding plans, the way we always told each other it was. We should have seen the signs sooner."

"It was ten years ago, Tucker. You're not still questioning yourself about it, are you?"

He said slowly, "Only because Lee's your sister."

They sat for a bit.

"You think a good relationship needs peace and quiet?" Was she agreeing, or arguing, or asking for something? She didn't have a clue.

Again, he spoke slowly, as if this whole conversation was a minefield he had to tread with incredible care. "I think if you can be quiet together and still feel like everything is perfect and right—" He stopped, then added impatiently, "But what do I know?"

"Well, I guess we do start to have a pretty good idea about that stuff by the time we hit thirty..."

Which is why it's killing me that we're sitting here like this. Connecting. We are! I'm not wrong about that. And yet there's this wall. He's pushing and pulling at the same time and I don't get it!

They sat without speaking, and none of it got easier or clearer. Daisy could hear Tucker's breathing, deep and careful now that it had returned to steadiness. She ached so hard to touch him. So hard. There weren't even words for it. It was such an obvious thing to do, after he'd told her all that he had. Just a hand on his shoulder or his thigh. A quiet lean against his body.

But she didn't. She couldn't. Because they'd been

through this already, out by the lake when she'd reached for him and been rebuffed. Because he would have done something about it if he'd wanted to signal a change. There was a preexisting and clear, if incredibly awkward, agreement in place. Not appropriate. Not right.

So why am I the right person, according to him?

The contradiction tied the knots inside her into tight, complicated twists—the fact that he could talk to her like this, tell her things he'd never told Lee even though they'd come within four days of getting married, and yet she'd put her hand on his arm a week ago and he'd taken it away.

And then he'd looked at her just now as if they could see into each other's souls with a single glance.

It didn't make sense.

They were just sitting there in silence, with the air so thick between them that she could practically taste it, and he'd talked about a man and a woman needing to know how to be quiet together, and it didn't make any sense at all.

Seconds passed. Or minutes. He muttered a few more disjointed words, apologies for doing this, for keeping her here. She made equally disjointed replies. It was fine, he didn't need to apologize, he didn't need to say or do anything he didn't want.

Then, just at the point when she really didn't know what to do next, because if she had to keep sitting here without touching him…without kissing him or him kissing her…she thought she might explode…. Somebody walked by with a pizza in a box balanced on one hand, and the smell of hot oil and garlic and fresh-baked dough hit them in a warm, enticing, wonderful wave.

Food. Nourishment. Comfort. Oh, yes, please! If she couldn't have a kiss, at least she might have a pizza. A little sound escaped her throat and her stomach growled.

Tucker, too, was watching the pizza box disappearing into the night.

"Man…" he muttered. "How long have I kept you here? That smells like we haven't eaten for a week."

"Mmm." Daisy suddenly felt totally drained of energy and light-headed from hunger, on top of everything else. She'd grabbed a peanut butter and jelly sandwich at around eleven this morning after a banana for breakfast, and hadn't eaten anything else all day. It was, what, nearly eight now? No wonder the smell of pizza had almost brought her undone. "You're right, I should get home," she said too abruptly. She began to rise, but it was her turn for unsteadiness now, and Tucker saw it.

He hissed out a breath, clicked his tongue and jumped up quickly to catch her elbow.

Just her elbow.

Just that one part of her.

"I'm not telling you to get home. That's not what I meant!" He swore under his breath. With a steely effort at control, Daisy willed the feeling of faintness away so that he didn't have to support her anywhere *but* her stupid elbow. "You're so hungry, you're about to drop," he told her.

Yes, but there was pizza. If she could get in her car and stop somewhere for pizza…

"Sorry 'bout that," she managed to say.

"C'mon, it's not your fault." He cradled her elbow— her stupid, inadequate elbow—in his cupped hand and bent his head.

"What's not my fault?"

"Nothing. Nothing is your fault." Once more the air between them seemed thick—thick with her awareness of all the places he wasn't touching her, all the ways it would be natural for him to hold her while she fully recovered her balance.

"That's good. I guess," she said.

"Yeah…"

"Confusing, but good."

"I'm sorry." He was leaning so close that she could feel the warmth of his skin in the air. Their lips were inches apart, but their eyes never met because she didn't dare to look up at him, and still the only place he touched her was her elbow. "I'm so sorry, Daisy."

"It's—it's okay, Tucker, seriously." She was letting him off the hook about something, but she didn't know what it was. "You can let go now," she told him after another moment.

He did, slowly, surrendering her elbow as if it was his passport at a hostile border crossing. "Sure you're okay?"

"Just hungry, like you said."

"I'm buying you dinner."

"No, you don't have to—"

"I'm buying us *both* dinner, okay?"

"Tucker—"

"Look, it's late and you're not the only one who'd kill for a pizza. I'll drop you back here for your car when we're done."

"That sounds too perfect to argue," she said weakly, and felt scared, suddenly, about how much she wanted to spend time with him at any cost, no matter what the deal, no matter that all he'd touched was her elbow.

I should have more pride. I shouldn't get swept along by so much emotion. I should have better boundaries.

But tonight, the pride and the boundaries just weren't there.

Chapter Ten

They found a pizza place not far from the hospital that Tucker said he'd been to before. It was family-run, not part of a chain, and had a sit-down section in back, beyond the front counter where it did a brisk business in takeout. "They do pasta and burgers, too."

"But I want pizza," she said firmly. She opened the menu and scanned the options for toppings.

"It was that guy walking past, wasn't it?"

"Sure was!"

"He doesn't know what a risk he was taking, out in the open with a box in his hand like that."

"Closest to mugging someone I've ever been," Daisy joked.

"You should have said," Tucker told her. "I would have been up for it. We could easily have taken him down, the two of us."

She laughed. "You think?"

"I could have pinned his arms while you grabbed the box. He didn't look like he needed that pizza nearly as much as we did."

"Tucker Reid and Daisy Cherry, the Robin Hoods of the pizza-thievery trade," she suggested.

"Except I'm not sure that eating it ourselves counts as giving to the poor."

"Mmm, true!"

"I think he got it from here," Tucker said. "The smell is the same. Mushroom and onion work for you?"

It sounded perfect.

And when it arrived, it was huge. They ate every crumb, having to lean over their plates and wrestle the giant slices with both hands. They had oil on their lips and cheese stretching in strings that needed to be scooped up and threaded into their mouths. With it, they drank tall glasses of sweet soda, scoring no points at all for healthy diet, but at the end of a difficult day, damn, it was good!

You couldn't get all tangled up in awkward awareness while you were eating pizza with your fingers, Daisy discovered. You couldn't hark back to emotions and stories from the past that maybe should never have been shared in the first place. It simply wasn't possible. The process was too undignified and too casual and too satisfying and fun. They talked about sports, instead, Daisy asking Tucker if he still had time for the skiing and hiking he used to love.

"Whenever I can, which isn't as often as I'd like. How about in California?" he asked her. "Was it the same as it is for me here? You wanted to get out there into the open air way more than you actually managed? Wait a minute, were you ever into those outdoor things the way Lee was?"

"No, not so much. I mean, I ski a little. I like to walk, but not places that require a backpack weighing me down.

San Francisco has some great places for walking. The Presidio and the Coastal Trail. Across the Golden Gate Bridge."

"And yet you always seem to have so much energy, just like Lee does."

"Different to Lee. I'm not as athletic. I'm just not. But I get bored if I'm not doing something, and if my creative side isn't engaged. I guess that's it. Lee's energy is athletic, mine's creative. Making something with my hands. Or appreciating what someone else has made. I'm loving the sight of the changes unfolding at the resort."

"You sit in the office, mostly."

"I have a ton of work to do on the new website, choosing the right photos and putting together some specials and packages that we've never offered before. In spirit I'm out there with the guys, jackhammering old concrete, because I can't wait to see how it's going to look."

"Your sister must be due home soon."

"The day after tomorrow."

"Will your parents come back up from South Carolina?"

"They're already on the road. They'll stay somewhere overnight and get here around lunchtime, if they stick to their usual plan. I wish I could have held them off for longer, but they want to see Mary Jane. Or that's the excuse, anyhow. I think what they really want is to micromanage my paving choices."

He laughed and leaned back, and she wanted to follow him with her body, lean toward him across the table until he changed direction and bent to her and smiled into her eyes and touched her mouth with his, right there at the table.

Need for his body drenched her like rain, so powerful

that she had to close her eyes while she suffered through it. She could not let this show. She must not.

When she opened them again, he was staring down at his fingers, clicking his nails together, while his whole face had tightened and narrowed.

"We should go," he said. "It's getting late. I'll drop you back at your car." He threw some notes on the table to cover the check, and when she tried to pay her share he just growled at her. "This one's mine, Daisy. You wouldn't even be here if it wasn't for Kyle's accident, which was my responsibility, not yours." He sounded so firm about it, or even angry, that she didn't object, just nodded in silence and picked up her purse.

Letting out a string of curse words inside your head was really not an effective strategy for getting unwanted physical responses under control, Tucker decided. Just get her back to her car, he coached himself. *Say good-night, polite and short and clean, let her drive away.*

It should have been easy. The visitor parking lot at the hospital was nearly emptied out, allowing him to pull up right beside her vehicle. She was supposed to hop out of the passenger seat, say a quick thanks and open her car door…

But this was Daisy, and she wasn't keeping to the script.

"I want to ask if there's any news on Kyle," she said as she slid her neat, pretty butt from his passenger seat. He could tell she was tired, but she was fighting it off, determined to do the right thing. "I'll see if anyone will tell me anything at the E.R. desk, or maybe Rebecca will still be around."

Hell, I hadn't spared a thought for Kyle.

Tucker had had other things on his mind, and once

again he cursed himself internally for the way his attraction to Daisy was messing with his priorities.

"Let me do that," he answered her. "I'll text you if there's any news."

"Maybe we should both go in."

"I don't know how much they'll tell us."

But they didn't need to go inside, as it turned out. There was a smokers' area near the corner of the building, and as they approached the main entrance they realized that the female figure standing there with hunched shoulders and a glowing cigarette tip was Rebecca. She recognized them at the same moment, stubbed out her cigarette and stepped toward them as they approached, her face brightening into a smile as she told them, "He's out of the coma!"

"That's great news," Tucker said.

"He's not talking yet, but he opened his eyes and squeezed my hand to say that he knew who I was." Her voice broke on the word and she dabbed at her eyes. "The doctors are saying everything looks good for a full recovery."

"That's wonderful."

"He's such an idiot."

"It wasn't his fault, Rebecca."

"It was, in part. Or it was his mom's. He didn't tell you he has epilepsy because he thought he wouldn't get the job if you knew. That was on Annette's advice. Of course. Never tell the truth when you can tell a stupid lie instead." Her voice dripped with sarcasm. "And then his medication ran out a day or two ago, and he didn't manage to get to the drugstore. He always leaves it till the last dose. I've told him not to do that. He asked Annette to pick it up for him, and she promised she would, but she didn't. *Of course,*" Bec repeated. Then she shook her head. "I could kill her. Why did he ask her and not me?

Hasn't he learned by now? I'd have been at the drugstore in five minutes." She gave another wry smile. "Sorry. Issues. Not your problem. The two of you, interrupting your date for this, I'm so sorry."

It wasn't a date.

Tucker could practically feel Daisy wanting to make the correction, just as he did, but neither of them said it. He didn't know if it was worse to let it go.

"I'm so glad it's good news," Daisy said instead, reaching out to give Bec's hands a quick squeeze. Bec squeezed back, and it was all so natural, the contact and then the letting go, and he felt almost crazy with envy and need.

Touch me. Squeeze me. My hands, not hers.

"I'd better get back to him," Bec was saying. "Annette didn't stay. Thank the Lord." She shook her head again and pressed her lips together as if fighting not to give vent to her complicated feelings.

Tucker understood. He'd felt that way in his teens over his father, and he felt that way now, about Daisy, everything inside him pushing and pulling in multiple directions at once. "Give us a report anytime there's any news," he told Kyle's girlfriend. "Text or call, whatever you need. We won't expect Kyle back at work until his doctors say he's ready."

"You mean you still want him back?" She seemed astonished, and tears filled her eyes once more. "I assumed you'd… That's so good. Not that I thought you'd fire him because of the epilepsy. But because he hadn't told you about it. Because he's such an idiot sometimes, when he listens to Annette instead of me. I just thought this would be your moment for letting him go. Thank you so much!"

"No problem, Bec."

"Please enjoy the rest of your date now!" She hurried back into the building without waiting for a reply, leaving the two of them with that awkward, mistaken word *date* hanging in the air, like the lingering echo of a musical note.

If it was a date, I'd kiss her right here, right now.

There was no one else in sight, no other smokers, no one making their way to or from the parking lot. Rebecca had disappeared. The automatic doors at the front of the building sighed shut behind her. Daisy was standing there, looking beautiful and uncertain and not warm enough in her thin embroidered sweater, her cold-stiffened shoulders almost begging for the warmth of his arms.

Why wasn't she heading for the car? Why was she just standing there? Waiting, as if...

I could do it.

And suddenly, it seemed achingly wrong not to turn possibility into actuality. Tucker just didn't have the strength or the will, and if there were powerful reasons to hold back, they had faded to nothing compared with the hammering insistence of his body. He could barely remember what his reasons were.

He hated that she thought he was rejecting her a week ago. He hated that he'd shared so much of his past with her tonight, while withholding so much more. He hated that he hadn't let her know how much he loved her company, her laugh, the mess and pleasure of sharing pizza when they were both tired and ragged at the edges but could still manage a few laughs.

And now she was waiting, looking at him with lips slightly parted and so soft and expectant, as if...

"I have to do this." The muttered words escaped him before he could hold them back, and hard on their tail came the action of his body. He bent toward her, reached for her, claimed her with a rough demand that reflected the fight and need inside him.

Before she could speak or react, he'd covered her mouth with lips that felt clumsy and half-numbed with the force of his desire.

It was a shattering kiss. Blind and hungry and with no room in it for questions. He held her face between his hands, scooped up the fragrant waves of her silky hair, gloried in the sweetness of her, felt the press of her breasts against his chest. He dropped his arms to tighten them around her body and just held her while his mouth discovered her.

None of it was enough. Not even her wild response was enough. She didn't hesitate, not for a fraction of an instant. A moan vibrated up through her body and her lips parted wider beneath his. He felt the questing sweep of her tongue and the movement of her hands. She laid them first on his back—softly, slowly running them up, then down. They reached his backside and rested there, cradling the bunched muscles of his butt with a sense of freedom and ownership and boldness that tore strips from his self-control.

She arched her back as if asking for his hands on her breasts and he obliged, cupping the neat, sweet shapes, feeling the hardened nipples that jutted against the thin fabric of her sweater and bra, before dragging himself away from the contact and wrapping her in a shuddering embrace once more.

They didn't even come up for air. He felt her begin to gasp in a lungful and then moan and press her mouth to his halfway through. The only way he could draw breath himself was to drag it in from her very skin, letting his mouth slip down to her upturned throat.

He wanted to keep going, down and down. Into the soft valley between her breasts. Down to the smooth stretch of her flat stomach. Lower still. He wanted to pull her clothes off and feel and taste and explore every inch of her. Where could they go? How soon could they get there? If this gritty wall behind his shoulders had been a bed, he just would have stayed and not stopped for anything. Hell, if it had been a kitchen floor or the staircase up to his apartment he would have stayed.

But it wasn't any of those places. It was a designated smoking zone outside a hospital on a chilly night, and this kiss was already hotter than a lighter flame.

Kiss too hot, location too wrong. There would be security cameras trained on this spot. Someone in a gray uniform would be out here any minute, demanding that they move on, get a room. Tucker couldn't stand the idea of bruising these precious moments with Daisy in such a way. He had to find a way to end this without losing it for good.

She sighed against him and took her mouth away, leaving her fingers laced together at the small of his back. He looked down at her and saw the darkness of desire in her eyes and the swollen satisfaction of her lips. "So why did I think I had it wrong?" she whispered. "Last week, out by the lake, I was so sure you were telling me—"

Hell!

His answering sigh grated painfully in his throat. "I was," he admitted, because it was time to start trying to make sense of this to her.

"You were?" She frowned up at him. Rightly so, because he wasn't making any sense at all, yet, and he knew it. The signals were all wrong. His ridged groin was still pressing against the front of her jeans, and he'd given her that ambiguous "I was."

He was *what?*

"I *was* turning you away," he growled, so it was fully clear. "You weren't wrong about that."

"So what's changed?"

She had him there. How did he do this? How did he pick his way through the tangle?

"Nothing has…"

"And yet we're standing here. In the smoking zone. Except we're not smoking. Or at least, not in the traditional sense." She was smiling. Or trying to. She still wasn't sure what was happening here and he couldn't blame her.

He tried to frame the right words, groping for them and second-guessing every one. "Listen, Daisy, I find you… incredibly attractive. That has to be obvious. But there are…a few things in the way." Mindful of the reality of those security cameras, he knew they had to let each other go, but he couldn't do it. Not yet.

"Things in the way? Like what?"

Ah, shoot, where did he start? After the way he'd dumped all that stuff on her earlier about his dad and Andrea and Jonah and his mom, could he really launch into another encyclopedia's worth of personal history?

He wasn't a big talker so much of the time. He didn't always trust words. They were too easy to fake and manipulate. On the receiving end of excuses from contractors, staff or clients when payments were late or things didn't turn up on time, the longer and more verbal those excuses were, the less he believed them. Would Daisy react the same way if he just went on and on?

"I'm married," he said.

"What?" She snapped back so fast that the movement of her body almost stung his skin, like getting pinged by an elastic band.

He added quickly, "At the moment."

"You're married *at the moment,*" she parroted, shocked and sarcastic at the same time. She wasn't a fool.

He was, though. "Wait, it's complicated, it's not what you think."

Shoot! Damn! In this situation, could there *be* a worse or more clichéd line?

"Oh, I bet it's not!" She laughed, turning on her heel at the same moment and breaking into a stride that was almost a run before he could reach out and stop her. "It never is!"

Would he have stopped her?

He was so tense, his hand landing on her shoulder would have hurt like a vise, which would hardly have helped. He'd blown this, big-time, no matter what he said next. Maybe it was for the best that she was practically sprinting into the parking lot toward her car, right next to his. The two vehicles looked lonely, standing there side by side, staring at the hospital with their blind windshields like a married couple who haven't spoken for a month.

"I can't leave it like this," he muttered to himself. As she ran, she had her arms folded protectively across her chest against the cold night breeze and it threw her off balance in her rush to reach the safe escape of her car. She looked angry and vulnerable and unhappy, and it made him ache with self-accusation and regret.

He went after her. Saw the uniformed security guards he'd been expecting. They exited the main entrance and looked at the scene unfolding in the parking lot. One of them approached close enough to say to him, "Everything okay here, buddy?"

"We're fine," Tucker answered. "Just emotional." Those guys would have seen way worse than this, he knew. They went back into the building, but he knew they'd keep an eye on their monitors in case it was a marital tiff escalating out of control. He forgot them and went back to beating himself up over his poor choice of words. Her reaction was hardly a surprise.

He caught up to her as she opened the car door and swung herself inside, and began his desperate attempt to pull them both back from the brink. "It's *not* what you think," he said, planting himself in the space between the car and the door she hadn't yet managed to shut. "It really isn't. You have to let me explain."

She twisted her head in his direction, her anger giving off a blast of electric energy that pulled on him as powerfully as their shared desire had done just moments ago. Her eyes blazed, bright blue now, when they'd been dark pools of heat as they kissed. "What, your wife doesn't understand you?" Her voice dripped sugar and acid at the same time.

"No—" He tried to lean down toward her, but the glare in her gaze made him pause and give her some space.

"You've been planning to tell her you want a separation but you're waiting for the right moment? Till the kids leave for college?"

"No, Daisy, c'mon!" He straightened in frustration and found himself looking helplessly around the deserted parking lot as if help might come—Mattie or Carla, maybe, to give him a character reference, tell Daisy what a wonderful brother he was and how it really was *not what she thought.*

"Okay, so you've just grown apart and agreed to live separate lives in an open marriage?" she drawled next, the sarcasm as thick as frosting on a cheap cake.

"Not that either. Can you please stop with the clichés?"

"You started them."

"I did. I didn't know what else to say." He leaned down again, ready to beg if he needed to. "If I'd started at the beginning, it would have taken too long."

"So start at the end," she retorted.

"Okay. The end is that we're getting a divorce."

"Isn't that another cliché? Does your wife know about the divorce, or will it come as news to her?"

"Of course Emma knows. It was in the plan from the beginning. Listen, I shouldn't have kissed you. I should have explained first. But we had an agreement not to get involved with anyone else—"

"We?"

"Emma and I. For Max's sake."

"Max, now."

"Her son. Sorry, it's complicated."

"That's another cliché, Tucker. It's always complicated, isn't it, for men like you?"

"There's no *men like me*. This isn't *like* that."

"And yet, you and Emma had an agreement not to get involved with anyone else. Which, I would have thought, is one of the traditional cornerstones of a marriage. Making it sound as if the whole thing is exactly *like that*. Which kind of brings us back to where we were before." She stuck the key in the ignition and he clapped his hand over hers so that she couldn't start the engine. She shook him off and tried to shut the car door, but his body was in the way. Painfully in the way, when she yanked the door toward her and it hit his shoulder, but he didn't care.

"We had an agreement, Emma and I, and I was fighting not to break that by getting involved with you. I lost the fight tonight, but the divorce is nearly through. Just a week or two more."

"I'll look forward to seeing the paperwork on that."

"And if you want, I'll show it to you. Look, I haven't handled this well."

"No…you think?"

"Believe it or not, I was trying."

"Hate to think how it would have gone if you hadn't been, Tucker." The sarcasm was light and bitter, and even in the midst of this, he felt the pull of her energy.

Arrgh!

He stepped back, intensely frustrated by his own inability to decide how to come at this, whether to tell her it was just the marriage that was holding him back. He didn't in all honesty know if that was the case. How could he tell her truthfully that everything would be fine as soon as the divorce was final, and that he had no other doubts? The sheer strength of what he felt filled him with doubt right now.

Ten years ago, one sight of her had changed everything, and yet where had it led? Nowhere. Was that where it would lead again now?

He should never have kissed her.

And yet he hadn't had the power or the will to stop himself.

A mess. Great. Just what he'd so much wanted to avoid. Just like his father.

The step back had been a mistake—one amongst many. It allowed Daisy to shut the car door, and she didn't waste the opportunity. In the middle of him trying to say to her, "Let's talk when we've had a chance to cool down," there was a slam and he knew she wouldn't even have heard beyond the second word.

She had the engine turning over in two seconds, and another two seconds after that she'd put it in gear and was pulling away. He had two choices, launch himself onto the hood or the roof like a character in an action movie, or watch her drive away.

He chose the second option. Told himself not to be stupid and melodramatic. This wasn't the end. They could talk tomorrow. They would talk, he'd make sure of it. In the meantime, he just had to work out what he was going to say.

Chapter Eleven

There was a familiar car parked beside the Cherry family residence when Daisy drove down the resort driveway in the dark.

"We got here today rather than tomorrow," her mom announced, stating the obvious.

"Why didn't you call and let me know?"

"We didn't want you to stress."

"Why would I have stressed?"

"Well, we didn't know if we'd manage to make the drive all in one day and we didn't want you to worry about the state of the site."

"Why would I have done that?" Daisy knew she sounded tetchy, but she couldn't help herself.

She was tired and angry and racked with conflicting emotions. She'd wanted to slump on the couch with the TV running mindlessly in front of her while she tried to sort through what had happened with Tucker tonight, and now here were her parents, and the last thing she needed was for either of them to guess that something was wrong.

"You might have felt you had to tidy it up for us. Because it looks a mess," her mom said.

"But I'm not worried about that. Of course it's going to look a mess at this stage in the work. Are you worried? Did you want me to tidy it?"

"We thought you might worry that we'd be worried." Denise came to a stop, hearing herself. She switched her slightly plaintive, anxious tone for one that was brisk and sensible. "You're right, I'm being ridiculous. Anyhow, we didn't call, and we're here, and we were slightly concerned that you weren't."

"You only just arrived?"

"Five minutes ago."

There was a beat of silence in the air as Daisy's parents attempted to recall that she was over thirty years old and that they didn't need to ask her where she'd been just because it was after eleven at night and she'd only just gotten home. They battled with themselves for several long seconds, won victory over their curiosity and maintained a heroic silence.

Daisy took pity on them. In any case, she needed to give them the news on Kyle. "The reason I wasn't here… We had an accident on site today, one of the Reid Landscaping crew. He had an epileptic seizure and fell into the pool and hit his head."

"Is he all right?"

"Much better than he was. He's regained consciousness and his family is with him." She skipped over the details of Annette and Rebecca and their hostility. "I've been at the hospital. Tucker was there, too, and it got late and we grabbed some pizza."

"Long day," her dad suggested.

"That's right. Sorry if I'm sounding like a witch."

"You're not, honey."

That was generous on their part. She was, and she didn't hold out much hope of improvement. Or not until she'd had some sleep, at least. She made a quick excuse and headed up to bed, then lay there with sleep a hundred miles away.

Tucker was married.

He'd kissed her and she'd felt as if she was in heaven, and he'd said those words *I'm married* and it had taken her straight to a kind of hell.

The problem with being thirty-one years old and single was that you'd heard all the variations on that theme, whether it was from your own experience or from listening to friends, or just from watching shows on TV. Some men thought that "married" was a very flexible condition, and there was always a justification, from their point of view.

Marriages did end. Tucker's was apparently on the point of doing just that.

If she could believe him.

Because some men lied.

Was Tucker that type? Her heart said no, but could she trust her own judgment when she knew how much it was impaired by the wild wanting in her body?

They'd kissed tonight. They'd *just* kissed, nothing more. In an unappealing public place, with the temperature twenty degrees lower than comfortable. And yet the kiss still burned all through her, kindling into life every time she thought of it, the way the embers of a forest fire sparked into life when the wind sprang up.

She could still feel his mouth on hers, feel the soft strength of his palms against her cheeks. She could still taste him, smell him. Her body still throbbed with need for him, throbbed with its insistence that this was *right*. Something that felt this good had to be right, didn't it? Right, and important.

Her body said so, her heart said so, and she fought not to believe either of them, because the loss of control was frightening. It reminded her of how she'd felt in the heady early days with Michael, as if her life was being swept along on a great powerful tide. It had been wonderful at the time, and it had ended in ashes, and she didn't want that again.

At four in the morning she was still lying there with the sheet twisted around her like a rope. Cursing, she straightened it out, got up and drank some water, came back to bed and felt sleep overtaking her at last.

It didn't last nearly long enough. After what felt like five minutes of oblivion, she heard her mom knocking at her door and calling her name, and realized when she took a bleary, one-eyed look at the clock that it was already after nine.

"Sorry I slept in so late," she croaked. She could hear the sounds of the workmen, but for once had slept through their arrival.

"And I'm sorry to wake you," Denise called. "You must have needed it. Honey, Jackie Bennett from the Reid Landscaping office is on the phone for you. Shall I tell her you'll call her back?"

"No, I'll take it." She struggled out of bed, opened the door and took the cordless phone.

"Hi, Daisy," came Jackie's voice, managing to sound both cheerful and apologetic at the same time. "We have a slight problem with the bricks for the barbecue area, and I'm wondering if you could possibly come in..."

"I'll be there in an hour."

And there is no reason to think that Tucker will be there, too.

He wasn't.

She dealt with the problem that Jackie had flagged. The company who made the decorative brick that was her first choice for the barbecue area had gone out of business, so she needed to make a new selection.

Fifteen minutes and it was done.

If she'd done it in fourteen minutes, she might have missed what happened next.

"Hey, Emma," Jackie said as the front door opened and a stranger entered. "Wow, it's good to see you!"

A stranger's face, but Daisy had no doubt as to who she must be.

This was Tucker's wife.

"Hi, Jackie, same back at you," she said in a crisp accent that Daisy couldn't quite place. Not American, definitely. English, maybe, but with a hint of something European and exotic in it. She was thin and brunette and model tall, very neat and chic and well groomed and Daisy hated her on sight.

It was a horrible shock to feel it—such a gut-level surge of ill feeling that shouldn't have been there but was, oh so powerfully.

"What can I do for you today, honey?" Jackie said to Tucker's wife with casual good cheer.

"Nothing. I'm not really here. Flying visit. Just had these papers to drop off." She placed a large envelope in a wire in-tray on the front desk that had Tucker's name on it.

"Are these...?" Jackie asked, suddenly alert.

"Yep. Earlier than we expected."

"Wow! Congratulations! I mean, I guess..."

Emma laughed. "Is that what people are supposed to say? You're sounding doubtful."

"I'm trying to find the right thing. You know I'd have preferred congratulations for a different reason."

"You're too much of a romantic. Life doesn't work that smoothly."

"It can," Jackie stated, sounding slightly aggrieved. "There's absolutely no reason why it can't."

"This is why I like you, Jackie, you're forty-one years old and you still believe in happy endings."

"And if you don't believe in them, then you need me in your life more than I thought."

"Actually, I'm pretty happy at the moment, celebrating a whole new chapter in my life, although if it's going to lead to a happy ending, I'm not so sure. Maybe just an interlude. I'm not feeling a need to tie myself down with that right now. I've been tied down for three years, for Max's sake, and that's what needed to happen. But let's..." Emma trailed off, a hand movement filling in the blank. *Let's not talk about this anymore.*

"Tucker's not around, unfortunately," Jackie said.

"That's okay, just make sure he gets these. Well, I know you will."

"Should I text him?"

"No, no need. Doesn't seem like the kind of thing you text or call about, don't you think?"

The two women shrugged at each other. Their mood seemed wry, almost bittersweet. Could these be the finalized divorce papers Tucker had talked about last night? They must be, Daisy decided, trying to stay calm. It made sense of everything they'd said.

"Anyhow, I must run," Emma said.

"You're not staying for coffee?" There was disappointment in Jackie's tone. The two women liked each other. Were friends. Daisy realized that Emma appeared in two or three of the pictures on the showroom walls, wearing shirts with the Reid Landscaping logo. She'd worked here once.

"I really can't." Emma sounded as disappointed as Jackie did. "I'd love to catch up, but I have someone with me." She gestured out to the parking lot, where Daisy could see the silhouette of a male head and torso at the wheel of a white car. As she glanced at him, he opened the car door and climbed out, as if he needed to stretch his legs. He began to look at the fall plantings that bordered the small parking lot. "Soon, though."

"Call me," Jackie suggested. "I can definitely tell we need to talk."

"Oh, we so do!" Emma agreed effusively. "Next week. Would that work for you? Lunch on Wednesday?"

"Perfect!"

"See you then."

She was gone in another moment, and Jackie turned back to her computer, straightening her shoulders as if to signal to herself and to Daisy that she was back at work. "Great, they've replied already, to confirm the order," she told Daisy, about the new bricks. "Delivery by Friday."

"That's great. Thanks."

"No problem. We'll be in touch if there's anything else, and I'm sure you'll see Tucker on site today or tomorrow."

Daisy managed an appropriate goodbye and could only hope she'd successfully hidden how shaky she felt about seeing—meeting—Tucker's wife.

Ex-wife, apparently.

Outside, the air hit her with a chill and she stopped on the steps to gather her control.

And to watch.

Be honest, Daisy, you want to watch. You're pretending to look for your keys, but really...

The man was still strolling around, but he turned when

Tucker's wife—ex—approached. Turned, grinned, put his arm around her, pulled her close and gave her a kiss on the mouth. She nuzzled against his neck for a moment, then looked up into his face and deep into his eyes, whispering something that made him laugh and kiss her again. After a moment, they broke reluctantly apart and climbed back in the car, and as Daisy crossed the lot to her own vehicle, they drove away. She didn't think they'd even seen her, they were both so lost in each other.

She felt so far out of her depth, her emotions like a rudderless boat being tossed in a storm, it wasn't funny.

Daisy wasn't back from the Reid Landscaping office when Tucker arrived at Spruce Bay. He knew she'd gone to the office because Jackie had let him know about the problem with the brick for the barbecue area, and had sent him a text just now to say, Problem solved. New order in. Delivery promised Friday.

Which meant Daisy would probably be back here soon. The knowledge put him on a hair trigger.

Denise and Marshall Cherry were here today, also, and keen to catch up with the changes that had happened since they'd been away in South Carolina. He felt hunted on all sides, even though he usually dealt well with nagging clients. Marshall and Denise weren't even that bad. He just wished they weren't here because when Daisy did get back, he really, really wanted a chance to talk to her and he suspected it wouldn't happen with extra people around.

Especially when those extra people were her parents.

Sure enough, when he saw her car, it turned directly into the lot in front of the resort office and she disappeared immediately inside, and he thought to himself, That's that, then. She's still just as angry as last night.

But she didn't stay in the office for long. He didn't realize she'd come over to the pool area until he heard a prompt from Brad—"Boss?"—and looked up to find her standing there all bundled up in a pink, red and cream fringed silk scarf and a padded jacket, its dark, smoky red bringing out the blond of her hair.

"Do you have a few minutes, Tucker?" Her mouth was tight and her eyes narrowed, but she looked tense rather than angry.

He straightened and dropped his tape measure on the ground, on full alert at once. "Sure, of course."

Marshall and Denise must be somewhere inside. Daisy didn't take him into the office or upstairs to their private residence—which he'd barely entered since his familiarity with it ten years ago—but began walking to the still-raw and uncompleted pathway that led down to the boat dock and the lake, moving at such a rapid, determined stride that for once the length of his legs was no advantage.

He followed her and had to say to her, "Daisy, if you don't slow down a bit and let me walk beside you, it's really not going to look as if we're just coming out here to consult about the paving."

Reluctantly, she dropped the relentless pace to a tense, staccato movement that was meant to look like a relaxed stroll. Even in the midst of the unspoken conflict between them, he couldn't help smiling to himself as he put the brakes on his own pace. She never did things by halves. The pink and red she was wearing seemed like the perfect colors for her today—passionate and rich—and he wondered if she'd chosen them on purpose.

"I saw Emma just now," she said as they came down the slope to the boat dock. "Your wife, Tucker."

"Oh, you did?" This wasn't what he'd expected.

"She was dropping something off at the office." She took a breath. "Tucker, I couldn't help overhearing. From what she and Jackie said, I think it was your finalized divorce papers."

"Whew, really?" This hit him in a way he hadn't expected. To be getting such news from Daisy, of all people. Today, of all days.

He was divorced. The chapter was closed.

If he believed in signs and omens... But he didn't. He clawed his mind back to the practicalities, while the cold that he hadn't noticed while he was working began to seep its way into his awareness. "She didn't call me. And Jackie didn't mention it."

"They seemed to think it wasn't something you talked about in a text message."

"I guess not. Those papers have come through sooner than I expected."

"That's what Emma said, too. I don't know if I'm glad I happened to be there, or not." They'd reached the boat dock. She stopped in the middle of the wooden planking and turned to him with an appeal in her face. "Tucker, please tell me the full story in a way that makes sense." The words ended on a whisper that had him watching the softness of her mouth like a man hypnotized.

He owed it to her to try to do it right this time. He owed it to himself to earn another chance at that beautiful, luscious mouth before he exploded with the need inside him. "Can you just listen? Don't say anything until I've said it all."

She pressed her lips together and nodded, and he knew it was acknowledgment that he wasn't the only one who'd handled things badly last night.

"Emma was working for me at Reid Landscaping on a limited visa arrangement. Her son was ill," he said. "Cancer. The same type that killed my dad. It's a lot more treatable in children, especially when it's caught early. But

Emma didn't have American citizenship and she was out of options for staying legally in the country. She didn't want to have to go back to England when Max was in the middle of treatment. She has no family or support network there. She's never really lived there, she's lived all over the world. There was really no place to go that worked for her. So we got married. It was actually Jackie's idea."

"Max isn't your child?" Her blue eyes still watched him, cautious, glittering, unsure. She wanted so much for all this to make sense, and the way she was hanging on his words almost made him start shaking. There was a massive *I want* in both of them, and he didn't know how much the sheer force of it would throw both of them off course, make rationality and clear thinking impossible.

"No, he's not," he told her. "Emma was divorced from his dad when Max was just a baby. They don't see him. He's from New Zealand, so that didn't help with her citizenship problem. Emma and I have never been involved, never slept together, never come close. You need to know that, and if you don't believe me, you can ask her. Ask her about any of this. Or ask Jackie."

"They're good friends."

"Yes."

"Why didn't you tell me this last night? Why, Tucker? If it's such a practical matter. If it exonerates you so completely from any kind of two-timing and deceit?"

"I meant to tell you. I messed it up. Started in the wrong place. I wanted to keep it simple."

"Is it simple?"

"I—I don't know. Feels simple today. For me. With the news about the divorce. Feels…"

But she didn't wait to find out how it felt, and he didn't have the words, not even in his own head.

Necessary.

Meant to be.
Impossible to deny.

She put her hand on his arm, the way she'd done out here last time, when he'd pushed her away. She was asking for a do-over because she was sure that things had changed.

And they had. She was right.

His divorce papers were sitting on Jackie's desk, while right in front of him stood the woman he'd wanted more than any other, for longer than any other, and if there was a reason not to respond to the soft invitation of her hand on his arm, he couldn't remember what it was.

"Oh, Lord, Daisy," he said raggedly, and slid her into his arms.

Chapter Twelve

If anybody was watching…

I don't care.

Tucker's kiss, Tucker's hard body against hers, Tucker's low voice whispering her name… These things seemed to fill the whole of Daisy's universe.

He'd been working this morning and his body felt warm beneath a blue work shirt that smelled faintly of concrete and dry leaves and healthy man. His thick hair was clean and silky and short as she ran her fingers through it. His arms and shoulders and chest were hard and firm with muscle in all the right places. But most of all it was his mouth against hers that claimed her awareness.

He drank her in as if he needed the taste of her purely to stay alive, and she just gave herself to it completely, closing her eyes, letting go of everything else. She didn't care if anyone saw them. She didn't care what was happening on the work site. His body felt strong and warm and already familiar. It felt like a gift, like a promise. Hers for the asking.

Soon, she was leaning on him for support because the power of this had made her weak. He deepened the kiss with a certainty and skill that left her trembling and made her mouth feel swollen with sensuality and satisfaction. How could a kiss feel this good?

And how long was it before they both realized they needed to stop? She had no idea. It felt like a minute, or like forever. He took his mouth away, loosened his hold, and she felt the cold air come between them until he took her hands in his, running his thumbs over her knuckles, making her instantly warmed once more.

"When can I see you?" he muttered. He pressed his forehead to hers, bumping it lightly. He leaned his jaw against her cheek as if he needed the support of her body the way she needed his.

"When...? I'll be in the office—"

"Not like this. You know what I mean. Alone. No one else around. Nothing getting in the way."

"Oh. Yes."

"Please."

"Soon. Whenever you want. Tonight." She had no shame about it because it felt so strong.

"Tonight, then?" His voice had gone so low, even a few feet away no one else would have heard. "My place?"

"Above the showroom, right?"

"Yes. Do you want to meet there, and we could—ah, hell—go out to eat, or see a movie or something?"

"Or stay in," she answered, too overwhelmed to pretend. "Just stay in? Could we do that instead?" Just as he did, she wanted privacy. Just the two of them. No one else.

"Stay in. Oh, wow, yes." He knew what she was saying, what she was offering. It hung between them, the promise of it so rich and real it almost made her gasp. Their two bodies tangled together, skin to skin. The smell of him all over her. Her hair brushing his chest. His weight on top of her.

"Yes," she echoed, because she didn't mind how clear it was.

He swore under his breath suddenly, and gathered her against his body once more, squeezing her as if he was feeling too full of joy to hold himself back. He was taut as a wire and eager as a child, raining kisses on her head, sliding his slightly roughened jaw against hers. "Just come when you can," he said. "I'll get in at around six, probably. Don't know how I'll get through the hours till then. I'll stop for something to eat for us on the way home."

"What shall I bring?"

"Nothing. It's fine. I'll take care of it."

"We'll see about that," she teased, her lips against his neck. "So I should come when?"

"Come anytime. Come whenever you want."

"I will. Oh, I definitely will." She laughed, hearing the double meaning in what he'd said, and he laughed, too. It was such a good sound, with something like triumph in it, all happy and male and proud. For sure, he wanted to make her come.

"We should get back," he growled. "I can't stand being this close to you and not being able to take it further."

"Oh, I know." She heard the breathlessness in her own voice and felt a dart of fear suddenly about how vulnerable she was making herself, how naked and raw. Tucker gave his own vulnerability back just as powerfully, in his transparent happiness about their plans, but should she trust that?

There was something else, too. This giddy, all-consuming rush of happiness felt familiar. The glow around everything. The perfection. The tide of feeling carrying her away. Wasn't this how she'd felt once before, two years ago, with Michael?

But Tucker kissed her again, as if he couldn't yet bear to drag himself away, and as they left the dock together she let go of the fear.

Don't spoil it, Daisy, not when it feels this good.

"Something in your in-tray," Jackie told Tucker in a carefully neutral tone when he checked in at the office for an hour in the middle of the day, before heading out to a potential new client in Saratoga.

Daisy had been right. It was the finalized paperwork for his divorce. He could tell by the return address on the front of the envelope.

Jackie watched him pick it up and weigh it in his hand, the end of his marriage in the form of a handful of papers. Her eyes were large and her mouth carefully closed. Happily married herself, she was in the same camp as Tucker's mom. She would have liked his marriage to Emma to turn into something real and lasting. It fit her sense of tidiness, and her sense of romance.

"Don't say it," he warned her now.

"I wasn't going to."

"But you were thinking it."

"Oh, you're keeping tabs on my thoughts now?"

"Ah, don't…"

"I can't help it, Tucker, I'm so fond of both of you, and it would have been so nice. I think I'm mourning this more than you and Emma are."

"I know you are! Emma and I aren't mourning it at all."

"It would have been so nice…"

"Call my mom, then."

"No need," she drawled. "Nancy called me."

"Oh, she's heard, then?"

"I think Emma must have told her."

"I'm surprised I haven't had her on the phone. Mom, I mean. Well, and Emma, too. I thought she might have called."

"Busy," Jackie said in a significant tone.

"Busy?"

"New boyfriend. He was waiting for her in the car when she dropped those off."

Wow. He felt the shock move through his body like the impact of a blow—a gut response on his part that rationally wasn't fair. The words slipped out anyhow. "What, she went to a bar and picked someone up half an hour after the papers arrived?"

"No, c'mon, Tucker, no need to say it that way."

"You're right. Ah...I'm sorry."

"I think it's been going on for a while. Emma talked about celebrating her freedom. Even though I'm disappointed you two didn't decide to go for the long haul, it was great to see her looking so happy."

"Huh." He didn't know what to say, or what to feel. His thoughts processed like a slow wheel turning, while Jackie watched him.

Okay, this was the heart of the matter—he'd been fighting this thing with Daisy, hurting her and confusing her in his striving to stick to an agreement with Emma that the latter had apparently forgotten all about.

He knew what Emma would say—that they'd already been divorced for a couple months in all but legal fact, that their original agreement not to get involved with anyone else was irrelevant now. Max knew about the separation, and understood that it wasn't a disaster or a tragedy, and that his life would go on in much the same way. He occasionally visited Tucker here at his upstairs apartment, but they were pals, not father and son. Max was in a much more secure, happy place in his life than he had been three years ago.

In other words, the original agreement between Tucker and Emma was obsolete, had been for a while now, and she was free to do this. And yet...

Emma had always had a thing about freedom that tended to assert itself at what Tucker considered the wrong times. The whole thing unsettled him, and he made the mistake of asking Jackie, "What did Mom have to say?"

"She thinks you're both going to regret the divorce. She's thrilled that Emma's seeing someone—"

"Oh, she's thrilled? That's weird!"

"—because she thinks he can't possibly match up to you, and Emma will realize what she's lost—"

"She hasn't lost anything."

"—and so will you, and in six months you'll be back together and planning a real wedding. Not to scare you or anything," Jackie teased, "but I think Nancy's probably looking at reception venues as we speak."

Tucker swore.

He felt the sheer joy and anticipation that had filled him since seeing Daisy this morning ebb away. He just wanted this to be simple, and true, and clear. He didn't want to consider that he might be doing exactly what Emma was doing—celebrating a freedom he hadn't had for three years. Or exactly what his father had done— pursuing needs and passions that left no room for the rights and needs and feelings of anyone else.

He wanted this feeling to mean more than that. Way more than that. But how could he know if it did?

"Don't worry about it," Jackie was saying gently. "And don't take any notice of silly, sentimental women, okay?"

"Like you?"

"Like me. You're a good person, Tucker. Trust that. Live a little. Enjoy yourself."

"There I think you have the right idea."

He shook off his unsettled mood and drove down to Saratoga, wishing he could eat up the hours as fast as he ate up the miles.

Tucker heard Daisy's car pull into the empty parking area in front of the building at twenty after six. The fall darkness had closed in an hour ago and he'd turned on the outdoor lighting as soon as he arrived home, not just the plain white lights that marked the route to the front steps and the stairs leading up to his apartment, but the carefully placed lighting in the surrounding plantings, as well. They made shadows and magic, and Daisy belonged with magic, he decided. She owned it.

Looking down as she climbed out of the car, he felt his pulse leap into action. This was the way he'd seen her that very first time ten years ago—getting out of a car, her hair catching unexpected shafts of light, while he watched unseen from an upstairs window.

For a moment, the idea spooked him. What was he looking for here? Some magic doorway into the past? Was there something unworkable and wrong about the way he responded to this woman? Was the timing all wrong, as it had been back then?

He just didn't know, and as he watched her, he decided not to care, not to ask any of those scary questions right now.

She wore a draped skirt in one of the intricately colorful pieces of fabric she loved as well as a wicked pair of black heels and a stretchy, figure-hugging black top with sleeves that came coyly to her wrists and a neckline that wasn't coy at all. As she moved around to the trunk of the car, opened it and leaned in, he saw the neat, enticing bounce and then the pale, shadowy swell of her breasts. Sheesh, he couldn't look away!

But then she heaved an enormous grocery bag into her arms and the sight of her body was lost to him. He wanted it back.

"Didn't I tell you not to bring anything?" he said to her moments later, when she reached his door.

"Yes, but I didn't say I was agreeing to that."

Still, it was just possible she'd gone too far, Daisy decided. She handed over the bulging bag of groceries—or would *supplies* be a better word?—and stepped into the warm, bright space of Tucker's apartment.

She'd been jittery and zingy all afternoon about their date, feeling like a schoolgirl and a princess and a cavewoman all at the same time—wildly crushy, the luckiest girl in the world, and desperate to be dragged by her tangled tresses into his primitive lair. She couldn't think about anything else.

"I won't be home to eat tonight," she'd told her parents.

Her mom had opened her mouth to ask about Daisy's plans, but her dad had cut her off very firmly. "In that case, Denise, why don't you and I go out somewhere, just the two of us." Her mom had managed to agree to this idea and had only needed one more piece of forcefully muttered coaching from her other half. "Don't ask, Denise. It's her life."

To escape her own turbulent feelings as much as her mom's heroically unspoken curiosity, Daisy had attacked the supermarket, initial plans for buying a bottle of wine and something for dessert soon turning into a basket that was almost too heavy to lift. Wine, mineral water, exotic juice mix and the ingredients for some kind of free form sweet treat that would be an exotic riff on tiramisu.

"It's not that I'm complaining," Tucker said, holding the bag, "but how long are you planning to stay?"

"As long as you want me?"

"Past your bedtime for sure." He put the grocery bag down on the side table and took her in his arms instead, and her body said, "Yes. This." And the schoolgirl-princess-Neanderthal feeling dovetailed into a sense of blissful, expectant calm.

You. Me. This.

"My bedtime might turn out to be very soon, I'm thinking," she said softly.

His dark eyes were alight and he was smiling a wicked smile filled with a blend of dizziness and satisfaction that echoed the way she felt. She wanted him to kiss her but he held back, watching her mouth with such a smoky look on his face that her lips felt the heat.

Instinctively, she darted her tongue out to cool the burn, and that was when he swooped, painting the touch of his mouth on hers then taking it away at once, teasing her so that she whimpered and he grinned.

"How could you do that?" she whispered. "Do it properly." She took his face between her hands to keep him where she wanted him and he gave her another swift kiss, gone too soon.

"Never heard of a place called delayed gratification?" he said.

"Heard of it. Never been there."

"I'll take you sometime." The whispered words brushed her mouth oh so lightly.

"But not tonight?"

"Not tonight," he agreed. "Not for another second."

The simmering kiss flamed between them as if it might never stop, and the grocery bag sat forgotten. He bent his head and trailed his mouth against her neck, her ear, her hair. He traced a line of warm contact around the neck-line of her top, lingering at the center V, where a push-up bra made the very most of everything she had.

Yes, she'd worn it on purpose, and yes, she didn't want him to stop.

He slid her top and bra strap off one shoulder and kissed her there, then did the same on the other side. She felt the soft slide of the fabric and then the warm press of his mouth. On her shoulders, on the slopes of her breasts.

She grabbed onto his hips, needing the contact and the support, needing to arch against his touch. Her top slipped lower, taking the black lace bra with it. He found her nipple with that hungry, seeking mouth and she gasped and he covered the tender skin in wet heat, caressing her with his tongue and lips until she was so sensitized she was primed to explode.

I can't bear it, it's too good...

The sudden dart of cold as he took his mouth away made her gasp again, as he found her other breast and gave it the same intense suckling pressure, while his thumb moved in slow circles over the moisture he'd left behind. Her breasts had never felt so cherished, so sensitive.

"Lift your foot," he said softly. He reached down, ran a silky caress against her thigh and down the front of her calf. She felt the hook of his finger on her heel and her shoe levered off into his hand. "I like these." He tossed the extravagant pump onto the floor with a clack, then said in a growl, "Now the other one." It went to join its twin.

He came back to her breasts, burying his face between them and cupping them in his hands, his big, work-hardened palms unbelievably tender and gentle while his mouth was exquisitely rough.

"Please strip for me," he whispered.

"And you. Else it's not fair..."

"Mmm." He wrenched at his shirt and flung it off in one long, twisting movement, then stood back and watched with bright, hungry eyes while she unfastened her skirt and slid it down. Bra and top went the same way, and all she wore were the matching lace briefs, deceptively modest. They covered her from low on her hips to the creases at the tops of her thighs, but the transparent pattern of the lace hid nothing.

He liked the lace. Still in his jeans, he closed the space between them once more and ran his hands over her backside, hooking his fingers inside the stretchy fabric and tracing the soft seam where her thighs and butt met. She tried to find the snap fastening at the front of his jeans, but he covered her hands with his and held her back.

At first she didn't know why. Weren't they supposed to be stripping? But then she heard the ragged whoosh of his breathing and understood. He was afraid of losing control too soon. Yes, he was that close. His hardness strained at the denim fabric and she wanted to set him free, but he kept stopping her, distracting her with the touch of his hands and his mouth and in the end he made it impossible for her to think of anything but what he was doing to her.

She barely knew how she'd reached the bed in the next room. He'd carried her or pulled her, or something, and she'd stumbled there with her hands still reaching for any part of him she could find. The big, hard knob of his shoulder, the soft skin above the waistband of his jeans. She fell back onto the satiny, puffy fabric of a comforter and he stretched her arms above her head and held them there with one hand while he ravaged her skin with his mouth, from her lips to her neck, collarbone, breasts, ribs.

Then he pulled at the black lace, stopping to explore its texture, his fingers whispering through the fabric against the seam of her wet core. She was on fire, so aroused that her patience fled and she lunged for him, wanting his whole body against hers. He groaned and gave in and they lay there side by side, twisted together. This time he was the one who fumbled for the fastening of his jeans, and moments later he was naked against her, hot and hard and so close to readiness that every breath was a groan.

She wanted him inside her.

He grabbed a packet from the bedside table, but then flung it back there and rolled away from her, fighting with himself. She tried to sit up, her body throbbing and her thighs slick with her own moisture. "What's wrong?" She trailed the tips of her fingers across his warm back.

"Nothing's wrong." He hunched himself at the edge of the bed. "Just want this perfect, that's all. Don't want to finish it too soon."

"It's not too soon."

"Says who?" He toppled her back again, and made his argument not with words but with touch, caressing and claiming until she was humming, writhing, whimpering, so close to the brink that she hadn't known it was *possible* to be this close without spilling over.

He had to give in. He had to give in right now. He had to take her and fill her and finish her this instant. She couldn't stand it if he didn't. She really, really just needed...

"Tucker... Tucker, please..."

He didn't answer. She ringed her fingers around his rock-hard length and felt him buck. Yes! She could tell how close he was, and how easily he would give in to the power of what she did to him. If she could just stroke him like this, draw him in with the rhythm and pressure—

No...

He pulled away from her touch and she had to chase him, roll him onto his back and straddle him and slide her hips and stomach against him, rub the hard peaks of her nipples across his chest. She wanted to ambush him now. She wanted to defeat his control completely.

She wanted to *make* him come inside her, even while he fought to make them both last longer. It had become a desperate, fantastically erotic game.

Who would win over whom, here?

Was the winner the one who lost control first, or the one who kept it?

Finally—*finally!*—he reached for the packet once more and she was so slick that he filled her effortlessly before she even had time to gasp. The sound that broke from her seconds later was part shudder, part moan, and she heard him groaning, too, as he bucked against her, over and over.

Seconds later, he took both of them over that trembling brink with such a surge that it lasted…oh, who even knew how long. It was simply a dark mass of movement and feeling and rhythm and crying out that left her breathless and weak and almost in tears.

Chapter Thirteen

They lay together almost without moving for a long time. There was just the rhythm of their breathing slowing and slowing, the soft tracing of his fingers on her hips and her mouth against his neck. Neither of them wanted to break this with words.

He spoke finally, his voice just a creak. "You falling asleep?"

"No…"

"You hungry, then?"

"Getting that way."

"Except I don't think I can move."

"Me neither."

So they lay there some more, until the soft tracings found a purpose, and her mouth stopped feeling lazy and began feeling full of need once more. This time the way they made love was so gentle and quiet that Daisy thought they'd both fallen asleep for a while, holding each other, her head pillowed against him.

She must definitely have fallen asleep because the way he touched and tasted her with his mouth felt like part of a dream. She floated on a billowing cloud of sensation and her climax surged over her like a wave on a summer beach. He entered her while she was still lost in it, bringing the intensity of her response still higher, breaking just moments later.

"I have to get better at taking this slow," he muttered, flung out beside her. They were holding hands.

"You almost killed me with taking it slow the first time."

"We can go a lot slower than that. You wait. You just wait. Give me a chance to refuel and then I'll show you."

He lunged off the bed and reached for his jeans, and she laughed at him for his sudden determination and energy. "You got something to prove, Reid?"

"I don't know. Do I? Let's find out." He stared her down, wicked and strong, his still-bare torso towering above her with all its smooth, tanned muscle, while she hadn't yet moved from the bed.

"Sounds as if I might need a little refueling also..." she answered unsteadily.

"Maybe we shouldn't bother to get fully dressed." He threw her a toweling robe from a hook on the back of the bathroom door, and didn't bother to put a shirt on, above the jeans. The robe was miles too big and she felt deliciously lost in it, wrapping it around her like a blanket, her skin still so sensitized against the soft swish of the thick cotton.

"And maybe we shouldn't bother with a lot of cooking," she suggested.

"I'm way ahead of you there."

He'd bought deli food for their meal, and it fit their mood. She helped him set it all out untidily on the coffee table—cheese and cold cuts and olives and cherry tomatoes, crackers and bread sticks, a bottle of red wine. They ate messily and hungrily, laughing at themselves, and she never put together her dessert. They just ate that the same way as the deli food. Daisy cut up cubes of cake and hulled the strawberries and they speared the pieces with forks and dipped them in cream and chocolate sauce and Irish cream liqueur.

What happened next was all too predictable.

They got in a mess.

Holding a forkful of strawberry and cream liqueur to Daisy's mouth, Tucker let it drip and the drips landed on her left breast and began to run down. He bent and licked them off, then looked into her eyes with an evil smile. "Sorry 'bout that."

"Can I be sorry, too?" She dipped a finger into the cream, ran it down the center of his chest and cleaned it with her mouth.

It escalated, and ended exactly the way they both wanted, and when Daisy finally crept into the darkened Cherry residence well after midnight, she didn't need her mom's sleepy voice coming from her parents' bedroom—"Glad you're home, honey, it's so late"—to tell her that she was in trouble, and not of the teenage kind.

She was home, it was late, and all she wanted was to be back in Tucker's arms.

Denise and Marshall drove down to pick Mary Jane up from Albany airport, and the three of them arrived back at Spruce Bay just before lunch. Mary Jane seemed giddily happy to be home, while at the same time she enthused about her trip and threatened to show hours of photos.

She'd celebrated her thirty-fifth birthday around a campfire in an African safari park, with the sound of lions roaring in the background. She had a light golden tan, and her medium brown hair had bleached in the African sun, with strands in the mix that had turned to white gold.

"Wow, I am so excited about what's been happening here!" she said, taking herself on a tour, which Denise, Marshall and Daisy all followed. "I love the bathrooms. Are they all done?"

"In the motel room wings," Daisy said. "But not all the cabins, yet."

"They're making good progress there, too, though," Dad added.

"So, we'll be able to start getting the rooms ready for opening, get all those plastic sheets off the furnishings, give all the rooms a good cleaning and airing?"

"We'll do it together, you and me," Daisy suggested, "with loud music playing. It'll be fun."

They all trooped upstairs to the family apartment, and Mom began getting out sandwich fixings for lunch, with Dad hunting down a new jar of pickles from the pantry.

"And the restaurant remodel?" Mary Jane asked.

"Priority is on the exterior work, before we lose the good weather. The restaurant interior is on schedule and close to being done."

Mary Jane announced abruptly, "We should open for Thanksgiving."

"You mean Christmas? Hasn't that always been—"

"No, I mean Thanksgiving." She seemed restless, suddenly, as if she needed activity to fight off the anticlimax of her arrival home. "We could do it, couldn't we? Not the whole place, just one wing of rooms and a few cabins. Advertise a renovation special, with a big Thanksgiving dinner included?"

"I suppose… It'd be tight. There's a lot to do." Daisy waited for one of their parents to chip in with their opinion, but they'd stayed very quiet during Mary Jane's tour. They were starting to let go of this place a little, and that was good.

"Let's," Mary Jane insisted. "I want to. I don't mind some hard work. We still have a few weeks. Let's do it."

"Well, let's think about it."

"No, let's make a commitment to making it happen, or else it won't."

Daisy decided not to argue. "Okay, yes, if you really want." If Tucker or any of the other contractors came up with a stumbling block, Mary Jane might be more prepared to listen to it once she'd unpacked and unwound and had some sleep.

Mary Jane moved to the other window. "I won't go into the grounds. It looks a mess. I'd get in the way."

"It's going to be great, though, Mary Jane. I'll show you the plans. Do you want to see—"

"Not right now." Mary Jane headed for her room and slumped down on the bed, her energy about the Thanksgiving plan already gone, while Daisy followed her and Mom began talking about getting a load of Mary Jane's laundry on before they ate. Dad had returned to his quest for the pickles, which were proving hard to find.

"Mom, I'm thirty-five years old, I can do my own laundry." She caught herself. "Sorry to snap. I'm pretty tired."

Daisy lingered in the doorway of her sister's room after their mom left. "Just tired, Mary Jane? Was the trip not all you'd hoped?" She looked more than tired, she looked dispirited and limp, and even the lingering glow of the African sun and her earlier excitement about reopening the resort couldn't hide it.

She sighed. "It was everything the brochure promised and more. I had a great time."

"Yeah?"

"And now I'm home, and it's over, and the only reason I go on all these damn trips is so I can pretend to myself that I have a great life, and I'm actually not a natural traveler, Daisy." She gave Daisy a beseeching look that said, *Please try to understand.*

"You're not?" Daisy said gently. "But you travel every year. Mostly twice."

"I get scared before I leave, and homesick a lot when I'm away, and half the time I'm only *telling* myself that I'm having fun because I know I *should* be. Maybe I should just stop. Give in."

"Well, yes, stop if you don't enjoy it. Give in, though?"

"Every year, I say to myself it's going to be my last trip, and then I start thinking about what my life looks like to other people. What it looks like to *me*."

Daisy knew exactly where this was heading now. She gave the only comfort that she could, saying gently, "You fake it pretty well, honey."

"I know, right? Mary Jane, the Traveling Cherry Sister. It sounds like a one-woman show. But I'm sick of faking it. Maybe I should just admit it. I want marriage. I want babies. At the very least, I want a travel companion sharing my bed. And I'm thirty-five now, and there's nothing on the horizon, and what if it's already too late?"

"You don't look thirty-five. Not now, with your hair all sun-kissed and that outdoorsy glow. You look gorgeous, even with jet lag."

"Yeah, but my eggs are thirty-five, and they can't fake it."

"You never meet anyone on your trips?"

"A few times, but it never feels real. It's always felt as

if we're both doing it because you're supposed to have a holiday romance. As soon as I'm home, it fades and doesn't seem to count, and since the guy is from Ohio or Illinois, or even Scotland, how do you keep that going unless there's a really strong sense of connection?"

"Ah, Mary Jane..."

"I don't expect you to understand this, Daisy."

"Why wouldn't I?"

"Because there's a huge difference between thirty-one and thirty-five. Because you lived in California for ten years. You didn't just...oh...stay on the family farm, like I did. You give off this sense of belief in yourself, Daisy— today you're practically radiating sunlight—and my eggs and I can't fake that, either." She wore a half smile that said she could mock herself, even when she was this low. Daisy thought this was a good sign, but had no concrete answers. Her sister was a terrific woman, but there were terrific single women everywhere.

She thought about Tucker.

Just thinking his name made her blush and heat up. If she and Mary Jane were having a heart-to-heart, should she confess what she'd done last night? And how she was feeling about it? And how maybe she wasn't a single woman now, and that might be glorious. She was so tempted.

Last night was amazing. I'd never realized chemistry could be so strong. But it feels dangerous, Mary Jane. What if it fades in a few weeks? What if I'm fooling myself, getting dazzled by things that don't count, the way I did before?

But would Mary Jane really want to hear that?

"Daisy? Did you hear what I just said?" Mary Jane queried impatiently.

"Oh, no, sorry..."

"You look like you're a million miles away."

"Mmm, yeah, the website. I've been…" Daisy let the sentence trail off, hoping Mary Jane would accept the vague explanation for the whereabouts of her thoughts. "But you were saying?"

"Trying to decide whether I should make myself stay awake until tonight."

"You usually think that's the best plan when you've flown west. You keep yourself awake, eat early, and you're conked out like a light before six o'clock."

"It is. You're right. I'd better get off this bed or it'll swallow me up. Six o'clock is sounding too far away. Maybe Mom's sandwiches will help." Mary Jane jumped to her feet. "I'm going to get that laundry on first so that Mom doesn't do it for me, then you're going to show me what you've done with the website and the menu planning, because if this Thanksgiving thing is happening, you're right, we don't have a lot of time."

Tucker sent a text message to Daisy as early as he decently could, after as long as he could make himself wait. When can I see you?

She didn't answer right away. He waited for ten minutes, pulled over at the side of the road, drinking coffee out of a paper cup and pretending to himself that he was taking notes following a site visit so that he could draw up an estimate for a new client.

But he was just going through the motions. He didn't think the client was serious, or realistic about a budget. You grew to have a feel for these things after a while. He added up the figures for his rough costing, based on what the client had wanted. Sixty-five thousand, give or take. No way they would go ahead, but he'd refine the estimate and email it to them anyhow. What did it really matter, when all he could think about was having Daisy in his bed again?

She still hadn't texted him back.

He felt irrationally impatient and jittery about it. Only ten minutes. Sheesh, it wasn't that he expected her to be hanging on her phone.

But it would be nice if she was, because he hadn't been able to get her out of his head for a minute all morning. He could smell her on his skin, feel her in his arms. She put a smile on his face every time he thought about something she'd said or something she'd done, or those moments when they'd licked chocolate and cream from each other's bodies, laughing about it because it was silly as much as it was sexy.

He wanted her in his bed again tonight and he felt selfish about it, and ruthless, and illogical. There was no room for patience, no room for sensible ideas about taking it slow, no room for her to have other plans.

Her sister was getting back today, he remembered.

Maybe that was why she wasn't checking her phone every five minutes.

He had a rush of irrational annoyance with Mary Jane for getting in the way, and he wished the trip to Africa was lasting another week at least. And while he was on that subject, he would have sent Marshall and Denise back to South Carolina if he could. And sent time-wasting clients to purgatory while he was at it.

He wanted Daisy to himself. He wanted their free hours to be just that—free and open-ended and answerable to no one so that they could see a movie and go to bed, eat out and go to bed, and laze around and laugh and talk plans and go to bed.

His phone sang out a melody, and he quickly touched the screen to bring up the new message. Daisy!

Tonight or the weekend? he read.

He texted back, How about both? and didn't care that he wasn't remotely playing this cool.
Sounds great.

Forget the texting, he wanted to hear her voice. He called her number and she picked up in about three seconds. Her voice was pitched low. "Tucker?"

"Yep, it's me."

Even lower. "Just a minute, let me close the door."

He liked the sound of that. Liked the sound of her breathing, because she'd kept the phone to her ear as she moved. "So, can I take you out, or something? Somewhere better than Joe's Pizza?"

"Hey, I had no complaints about Joe's Pizza..."

"You know what I mean."

"I do."

"I'll make a reservation and pick you up, okay?" He wanted to spoil her. He was already combing through the possibilities in his head. Lake views and candlelight, or maybe music and the sizzle of steak.

"Mom and Dad and Mary Jane will all be here," she said, with doubt in her voice.

"Does that matter? Oh, you mean...is your family having a welcome-home dinner?"

There was a second's pause, then, "No, it doesn't matter. We weren't planning anything special. Mary Jane has a mother lode of jet lag. It always hits her pretty bad. She's going to be sound asleep by seven. You're right. It doesn't matter who's here." She laughed, as if this was a delicious idea.

"Seven, then?"

"Seven," she agreed, and made one simple word sound like an erotic promise.

"Dress up," he blurted out, thinking of lacy underwear beneath silky fabric.

"Same back at you, buddy. The work shorts and flannel shirt are pretty hot, I have to say, but I'd like to see what else you got."

"Oh, I got plenty."

"I know. I saw."

"You did…"

"I tasted."

They ended the call and he wondered why the phone hadn't started to smoke.

A surge of energy and joy flooded through him so powerfully that he had to fling open the car door and get out, purely so the energy would have somewhere to go. The air smelled so fresh and good with its tang of autumn pine. The sky was so blue today, with a pattern of cloud just starting to pass across it, suggesting a change in the weather. He could hear a stream rushing in the woods, hurrying to reach the lake he could glimpse through the trees, whose near-bare branches looked as graceful as a woman's limbs. The sound of the water was like wild music.

Man, he wanted to run or dance!

Instead, he yelled. Whooped like a sports fan or a cowboy.

"Whoo-oo! Yee-ha!" Then he just laughed. At himself. At life. At the driver of the car tooling past, who looked at him as if he needed a straitjacket.

So this was happiness. Your voice carrying and echoing in the cold air. Your body with energy to burn. Your heart aching with happiness and threatening to burst out of your chest. This was what it did to you. It made you crazy, and you didn't care about a thing.

Back in the car minutes later, he called the Adirondack

Steak House and made a reservation purely because it had the darkest corners of any restaurant around here that he could think of, and if he wasn't eating with Daisy tonight with a little darkness for safety, he thought he might get arrested before the night was out.

Chapter Fourteen

"I won't be home to eat tonight," Daisy announced at around six o'clock. She'd thought about waiting until Mary Jane hit the hay before saying this, but that seemed sneaky somehow, and after the naked phone conversation with Tucker she wasn't about sneakiness.

He'd made it so clear how impatient he was to be with her, and she felt the same, and why hide it—from each other, or from anyone?

Her parents and Mary Jane would all have to know soon enough, so why not now?

The three of them looked at her, and she could see her mom trying hard not to ask the obvious question. Time to put her out of her misery.

"I'm having dinner with Tucker. He'll be picking me up."

"Dinner?" Mary Jane said.

Mom and Dad stayed silent, and Daisy could see them

reaching the correct conclusion. She'd been with Tucker last night also, and the night before.

"It seemed like a nice idea," she told her sister lightly.

Mary Jane nodded slowly, and the word *date* hung in the air, unspoken.

After a moment, Mary Jane stood up. "I am too tired for this tonight," she announced. "But, Daisy, have you told Lee?" She didn't wait for an answer, just stood up and headed for the door. "I'm going to bed."

"And I'm going to go through that final box of papers," her dad said.

Mom waited until both of them had left the room, and until their two sets of footsteps had faded away in opposite directions. She had more to say. This much was clear.

"Daisy, I have to ask… I didn't want to say anything in front of Mary Jane… She always seemed the one most angry with Tucker for the breakup with Lee…"

"She would say that that was you and Dad."

"Well, yes, at the time, maybe, but as soon as I'd been to visit Lee in Colorado and seen how happy she was…"

"So what is it that you have to ask, then?"

Her mom sighed. "Just…are you sure you know what you're doing?" She spoke quietly because Marshall was only in the next room.

"No. I'm not sure at all." She paused. "Why do you think Mary Jane was so angry about the whole thing? Was it Alex? Was she channeling her own situation?"

"I don't know, honey. There were things she didn't say. When you and Lee both moved away, Dad and I were so thankful to still have one daughter close and committed to Spruce Bay, but I wonder now if we should have discouraged her from staying on here. I'm not sure how we'd have run the place without her, but maybe that was the wrong priority."

"She loves it here. She's such a good manager for a place like this."

"Still…" her mom said.

"Still…" Daisy agreed. "When are you and Dad heading down South again?"

"The day after tomorrow. We won't be back again until Christmas, and then just for the holiday. This shuttling back and forth, not really living in either place, is getting old pretty fast. So you and Mary Jane will be opening for Thanksgiving and then the winter season on your own."

"We'll get our teeth into it. Mary Jane knows what she's doing."

"And *have* you told Lee that you're dating her ex?" Mom asked quietly.

"Not yet," Daisy said. "I'm not sure there's anything to tell, is there? I talked to her about hiring Tucker's company before we met for the initial consult, and she was fine about that."

"There's a difference between contracting him and dating him."

"And there are a lot of steps between seeing someone and getting engaged." She hated the idea of telling Lee. She remembered the way she'd gushed to her about Michael, and couldn't imagine saying those things about Tucker. Spilling it like that. Opening her heart. It just felt wrong.

"Don't put it off too long," her mom said.

"I won't," Daisy promised, because *too long* was a very inexact measurement, after all.

After Mary Jane's room had gone dark and quiet, Daisy took a shower and changed, appearing in the family kitchen at ten before seven. Standing at the stove making spaghetti for herself and Dad, Mom immediately went wide-eyed at the sight of the slinky black dress, killer heels, smoky makeup and glints of jewelry. "Wow. You really are going out to dinner!"

"Yep, I sure am," she answered, deliberately flip.

They heard a car coming along the main driveway.

"Um, say hi to him for me, then," Mom said.

"I will."

She said a quick good-night to her dad, then hurried down the stairs and out the door, heart already beating faster, wanting to meet Tucker before he could park and get out of the vehicle. She wanted nothing to spoil this, and the wariness in her parents' eyes certainly had the power to do that.

As she slid into the seat beside him, she saw the way his eyes went dark at the sight of her. "You look amazing." He leaned across and gave her a velvety kiss laden with the promise of more. He smelled wonderful, clean and male and tangy. What was it about a man's warm skin? *Tucker's* warm skin?

The dark interior of the car was like a cocoon as they drove. The weather had turned colder, with the possibility of light snow in the forecast. You could smell it in the air, and the cold tingled in your nose, but here in Tucker's car they were warm and quiet and together. Neither of them spoke much. Daisy simply hugged this precious feeling of unity and kept herself in the moment.

"Where are we eating?" she asked.

"The Adirondack Steak House."

"It'll be pretty quiet tonight."

"That's the plan." He glanced across at her, a sweet, wicked grin breaking onto his face. "Quiet corner of a quiet restaurant. *Dark* corner."

"Ooh."

And when they were seated, he kissed her across the table before their menus had even arrived.

They were lost in each other for the next two hours, talking about everything and nothing, laughing out loud and then dropping unexpectedly into stories from their past. Daisy told him about her year in Paris, about how it felt to make perfect desserts for a hundred people. Tucker told her about the lean years when he'd first gone into business for himself.

"It was just me and one other guy, no office. I worked out of my truck. That truck was my biggest investment. Brand-new, professionally painted signs on the sides. Because I knew if I showed up in what I could *really* afford to drive, which was some clapped-out old pickup with a hundred thousand miles on the clock, no one would hire me."

"Now you have how many trucks?"

"Four. And even if a couple of them have a few miles on them now, they're repainted whenever they need it."

"First impressions, which is just what you're doing for us at Spruce Bay, with the landscaping."

"First impressions… They're pretty important." He gave another slow grin. "I wonder if I should tell you—"

Their steaks arrived, both of them still sizzling on black metal platters, with the aromas of freshly poured mushroom and pepper sauces rising with delectable intensity into the air. Daisy leaned over hers and inhaled as it was placed in front of her, and she could smell the gardenia and wax of the white scented candles, as well.

She looked across at Tucker. He was leaning back, his eyes in shadow and his mouth very soft. There was the tiniest suggestion of a frown creasing his brow. "You wonder if you should tell me…?" she prompted.

But he shook his head. "Doesn't matter. Not important. Not today." He added something else under his breath that she couldn't catch, then said in a different tone, "Tell me about the new menu for the restaurant at Spruce Bay."

The steaks were tender, juicy and delicious, and they lingered on for dessert and coffee until they were the only ones left. On the way out to the car, Tucker asked her lightly, "So...my place?"

"Yes, please."

"That's what I wanted to hear." He pulled her close and squeezed her, and they walked with their arms around each other and their hips bumping, and had to stop before they reached the car, because it had been a whole ten minutes since they'd last kissed.

"We're never going to get to your place if we keep getting distracted like this," she whispered against his mouth.

"This isn't the distraction. This is the whole point. The driving part is the distraction."

"It's quite a big truck," she said, only half joking. "And quite a dark parking lot."

"And quite a cold night," he pointed out. "And starting to snow."

He was right. The first feathery flakes began to spiral down. They broke contact and ran to the vehicle hand in hand, then drove through a white whirl and reached his apartment with snow caught in their lashes and china-cold cheeks.

They soon warmed up.

In the best way possible.

Tucker stripped fast, pulling his shirt over his head so that Daisy had to stop to look at what the action did to his ripped body. She shimmied out of her dress, then saw that he'd done the same as she had—paused to take a look. They grinned at each other, and Daisy felt a balloon of such intense happiness swelling inside her that it almost hurt.

"You're still cold," he muttered.

"So warm me up," she whispered back.

"Like this?" His big body spooned her from behind, and he stroked her wherever he could reach. Her breasts, her hip, between her thighs. "It's not cold here..."

"No, far from it."

They stopped talking, and the heat began to radiate outward from where his fingers stroked her. It sizzled across her skin, it throbbed deep within her, it wrapped around her in the form of his arms, it filled her as he turned her and pushed inside her, hard and velvety and groaning his impatience.

Their need for each other was so powerful that it almost made her cry. She had to cling to him, pressing her mouth into his shoulder, feeling their shared climax like an ocean wave. She didn't even know which direction was up. All she could do was breathe and feel.

When they lay still again, spooning as before, he was more tender with her than she'd known a man could be. "Okay?" He moved strands of hair from her eyes and mouth with fingers that moved like delicate brushes. Tucking one behind her ear, he ran a fingertip around the sensitive edge, down to the lobe and then to the soft valley between her neck and jaw.

She whispered, "So okay, I can't even tell you."

He brushed her breasts lightly, letting his hands wander as if they just wanted to explore for hours. His breathing had slowed and deepened. She could feel the movement of it against her back, so intimate and quietly strong. "Was amazing, wasn't it? Was...mmm...just amazing."

"You got nothing better than *amazing*?" she teased.

"Nope. Nothing."

They both slept. Daisy was the first to awaken—sleepy, happy, sated. She could see the numbers on the bedside clock, reading 2:17 a.m., and was lazily surprised to find it that late. She'd slept so soundly in Tucker's arms. How long since she'd last fallen deeply asleep this way, and awoken to such a feeling of perfect contentment?

Well, Michael.

She remembered.

Wished she didn't.

They'd been out to some lavish charity event, where he'd seemed to know everyone—celebrity chefs, Hollywood stars. She'd been dazzled at being in such company, overwhelmed at being chosen by a man like this, a man who moved in these circles, and had disappeared into the huge and gorgeous ladies' powder room a couple times to text friends, and Lee, *You would not believe who I just met!!!...I am having the most incredible night.*

Michael had taken her back to his place afterward, and they'd made love without a false move or a second of silliness, and she'd fallen asleep, woken just the same way she'd awakened now, in the arms of her lover.

She'd stroked Michael's smooth chest, registering for the first time that it had been waxed to remove every hair. Well, this was California. Most men probably did it...

Then she'd realized that Michael was awake, too, and watching her with a sleek smile, and in the spill of light from the street outside, she could see the self-satisfaction in his face. She was a lucky girl, to be in his bed like this, and he was clearly quite sure she knew it. "Get me some water, could you, lover?" he'd asked.

That was the moment when the first chink of doubt had cracked the facade.

"You okay?" Tucker was awake also, and didn't realize that there were three of them in the bed—himself, Daisy and her memory of Michael.

"I'm great."

No chink of doubt tonight.

But she was spooked by the memory. Was there any difference between how she felt about Tucker now and how she had once thought she felt about Michael?

There was.

There *was!*

How did you truly know...?

"Can you please take me home?"

"You don't want to stay?" He stretched an arm and pulled her even closer against him, instantly giving her twenty reasons why she should.

"I really, really want to stay, but I—I'd better not. Not tonight."

She needed some breathing space. This was so scary good that she didn't trust it, didn't know how to trust it, after Michael. She had to get her feet back on the ground, because real feelings didn't float like this, did they?

"Really?"

"Yes, really." Daisy dragged herself from the bed, and Tucker watched as she began to dress, his face hard to read. She gave him a prompting glance, and said with a tease, "What, you're going to drive me home naked?"

"Nah, I'm getting there." He rolled to his feet in one movement and grabbed a pair of jeans and a shirt draped over the back of a chair. He was fully dressed and sticking his feet into running shoes without undoing the laces, while she was still working on the zipper at the back of her slinky black dress. "Let me help you with that," he said, and the feel of his body standing behind her and the deliberate caress of his fingers as he slid the zipper up almost brought the whole driving-her-home plan undone before it had even gotten off the ground. Was he doing it on purpose?

Almost brought the plan undone, but not quite. She

took control of herself and stepped away from temptation, hugging her arms in front of her body for self-protection. "I really don't want to be doing the walk of shame tomorrow morning in this dress, with raccoon eyes, Tucker."

"You can take care of the raccoon eyes," he teased. "I do have a bathroom."

"I know, but..."

"But? C'mon, Daze." He gave a slow grin, wickedly tempting. He knew it was tempting, damn him, and she could tell how much he wanted to win this. And how much he was sure that he would.

She hardened her resolve. "I just think I need to get home. It's late enough already."

He was disappointed, and he couldn't quite hide it. Even though he didn't say anything, Daisy could feel the slight change in his mood. He thought she was being ridiculous, acting like a teenager scared of being caught out after curfew. He was wrong, but she couldn't give him an explanation. How could she?

I love being with you so much, I'm scared I might burst. And then I'm scared the bubble might burst and there'll be nothing left. It happened before and it was so horrible I get sick to my stomach when I think about it.

They went down to his car. The snow laid two inches deep on the ground now, but it had stopped falling. There had been very little traffic on the roads tonight, and when they turned down the Spruce Bay entrance driveway, after a largely silent journey, Tucker's pickup made the only tracks through the pristine white. The tracks would tell their own story, come morning, if anyone cared to examine the evidence.

He pulled up in front of the office, turned off the engine and looked at her. She knew he was angry. Not so much angry, the feeling wasn't as strong as that. Frustrated. Disappointed. Not seeing it her way.

It felt horrible, and she didn't know what to do. So she did the only thing that seemed possible. She kissed him quickly, then asked upfront, "Again? Soon?"

"What time will curfew be?"

"It's not that."

"Then tell me what it is. Here I am, sneaking you home in the middle of the night. Are you going to climb through your bedroom window? Take off your shoes on the porch so you can creep inside in stockinged feet? Is your dad going to be standing there with a shotgun pointed at me?"

Oh, crap!

"Nothing like that."

"Isn't it? Isn't it because of what happened ten years ago?"

Okay, maybe that was a part of it, too. Tucker had already broken up with one Cherry sister. Would it end up being two? She didn't want to put her family through another mess. She didn't want them thinking it was Tucker's fault.

"Maybe a little," she said. "I want to ease them into it. Which is probably me more than them, but…no, it's them, too."

"It's Mary Jane."

"Yes, it is. How did you know?"

"Ah…just a gut feeling. She disapproves."

"No, Tucker, she's *lonely*."

"Lonely?"

"We talked about it today. She wants a husband, and babies, and not to be going on all these exotic trips on her own. But please don't blame Mary Jane. It is me. I… need time."

"You can have time, as long as you spend it with me."

He was trying to joke about it, but the words came out sounding a little too forceful.

"Tucker…"

"It's okay, you don't have to say anything." He let out another sigh and pressed his fingers into his eyes. "That was me in bulldozer mode. Sorry."

"Let's forget this whole conversation." At almost three in the morning, neither of them needed to argue anything out for long.

"Let's. I'll call you," he said. "We'll ease into this…"

"But let's make it fast?"

He gave a reluctant grin, there in the snowy dark. "You got me," he said. "I have no patience."

"I like that. Mostly."

"Get out of this truck before I make a grab for you and we're right back where we started."

She was still smiling as she let herself into the house, using the office entrance. Tucker waited until he saw the door swing open, then started the engine and circled the truck around, making another loop of fresh tracks in the snow. She waved at him, but couldn't see if he was waving back.

Didn't matter. She kept smiling anyhow.

Then noticed that there was a light on upstairs, in the family living room. Going up, she heard sounds in the kitchen, and there was a light on there also. Mary Jane was making herself coffee.

"What are you doing up so late?"

"You mean, what am I doing up so early? I slept for nearly nine hours." Mary Jane added deliberately, "Then I heard Tucker's truck."

"Your window doesn't look out onto the front. How did you know it was—"

"Oh, please, Daisy! I went along the landing and looked

out the end window and saw the Reid Landscaping logo on the side. And, no, I didn't keep looking, I came back here and got the coffeemaker started. Want some?"

"No, thanks."

There was a short, awkward silence.

"You didn't tell me it had reached that point," Mary Jane said quietly.

"What point?"

"Oh, don't make me say it. The point where you come sneaking in at three in the morning, all scrambled into your clothes."

"Do you mind?"

"Of course I mind."

"Because it's Tucker?"

"Because it's anyone." She made a stricken sound, impatient at herself. "Yes, because it's Tucker. Because he's been waiting—" She stopped and shook her head. "Doesn't matter. Sorry. Believe it or not, I do know this is largely my problem, not yours. When are you going to tell Lee?"

"Soon. Sometime. When it feels like it's gotten to that point."

"Don't you think it's gotten to that point already?"

"Can't you let me be the judge of that, Mary Jane? Can't you trust that I care about Lee as much as you? And that I need to have the right handle on where this relationship is going before I talk to her about it?"

"You mean, you think it might not last?"

"How can I know? It's so far lasted about a week. Where's its track record? Where's mine? Are you really asking me to search my soul about this now, at three in the morning?"

"No, okay, I guess not. Go to bed."

"Only if you promise we're good."

"We're good. It's not your fault." She turned back to the coffeemaker with a stubborn look on her face, and all Daisy could do was say good-night and go to her room.

Chapter Fifteen

"Tucker, do you have a minute?"

"Well, I'm in the pickup, pulled over on the side of 9N," Tucker told his mother at the far end of the phone. He'd finished the final check on a completed project at a bed-and-breakfast in Lake Luzerne and was counting the minutes until he arrived at Spruce Bay.

After some intensive work, there were only a few tasks awaiting completion, and the Reid Landscaping crew's focus had largely moved to their next job. Kyle was back after his accident, his attitude much improved and his conversation littered with Rebecca's name far more than previously. With Marshall and Denise in South Carolina, Daisy and Mary Jane had been working like dynamos on readying the place to open on a limited basis for Thanksgiving next week.

"So you can swing by?" On the phone, his mom sounded eager, confident and a little concerned.

Tucker could read that voice. She really needed and wanted him to come, and was sure that he wouldn't let her down. "What's up?"

"Oh, nothing really... I'll explain when you get here."

"Because you're so sure I'm coming."

"You never let me down, Tucker, I hope I know that by now."

A neat piece of emotional blackmail, he noticed. She didn't resort to it very often, but when she did, he was a pushover for it. Okay, yes, he was a good son. He hadn't let her down in the past, and he wasn't going to start now.

"I'll be there in twenty minutes," he said, hoping it was just a leaking washing machine or some insurance papers she needed him to look over.

It wasn't.

Pulling up in front of his mother's house, Tucker saw Emma's lime-green metallic-finish car parked in the driveway. They'd only seen each other once since their divorce had been made official, when he'd taken Max to a movie ten days ago. Now Max met him at the door, lunging at him with total trust. He knew Tucker would scoop him up and give him a swing through the air, and Tucker obliged. "What are you doing here, buddy?" he asked.

"Just hanging out with Nancy. Mom was busy."

"Oh, Nancy was taking care of you?"

"Just for the afternoon. Mom's here now, to pick me up."

"Yeah, I saw the car."

"They're in the kitchen."

He went through, steeling himself for the two women to present a united front in whatever this was about. Emma greeted him with her usual brief hug, her cheek carefully turned for a token kiss. Her eyes were a tiny bit pink around the rims, and he had about four seconds in which to wonder if she'd been crying. She was one of the few women he knew who looked pretty when she was in tears.

There were two empty coffee mugs and a milk glass on the café-style table in the kitchen, as well as a plate dotted with cookie crumbs. Something was brewing in here, and it wasn't just Colombia roast.

His mom didn't waste any time. "You don't have plans this evening, do you, Tucker?"

"I might," he said cautiously.

It was the truth. He and Daisy didn't make plans anymore. They made assumptions, and he was making the usual one right now—that they'd spend the evening together. Tonight it would most likely involve eating Thanksgiving recipes a week ahead of schedule. Which was fine. If he was with Daisy, that was all that mattered.

She'd softened on the subject of spending the night at his apartment, and that need for space that she'd talked about at three in the morning a couple weeks ago had seemed to fade. If he was bulldozing her, then he was pretty sure she liked it.

He liked it. He had endless energy for this, so much that he couldn't imagine her not feeling the same. Life didn't work like that, did it? When one of you felt this strongly, the other one did, too.

"Oh, good!" Mom said, instantly translating "I might" into a straight out "No plans at all."

"What's happened?"

Mom spread her hands. "I don't know how to start."

"It's fine, Tucker," Emma said. "It's really not a huge deal."

He didn't usually hear her accent anymore, with its odd mix of British and South African and something else, but tonight it jumped out at him. Cute. Exotic. She did do that deliberately, he knew. She put the accent on a little stronger when she wanted something. He didn't know if she was even aware of the affectation, it might be entirely unconscious, and normally he found her so transparent that it didn't bother him. He'd never felt manipulated by her because he'd only ever acceded to her wishes when they made sense.

"Just tell me."

"Emma and Rob have had a fight," Mom summarized.

"Not a fight, Nancy," Emma corrected quickly. "Tucker, we had a bit of a tiff. We were supposed to be having a family night with Max today. The go-karts at Lake George, then pizza and popcorn and Max's choice of movie at home, but Rob has business in the city tomorrow and he decided to fly down this afternoon."

"For a start, who's Rob?" Thanks to Jackie, he could make a pretty good guess, but he was feeling stubborn and resistant, facing his mother and his ex-wife like this. They were both looking at him with big eyes, turning him into their knight in shining armor, but the only knight he wanted to be right now was Daisy's. He hadn't seen her since six o'clock this morning, and that seemed way too long.

"Emma's been seeing him for a couple months," Mom explained.

Tucker thought about mentioning his agreement with Emma that they wouldn't get involved with anyone else until their marriage was over. He thought about asking why he was apparently the last person to know, and why nothing had been said ten days ago when he'd taken Max to the movies. He thought about probing a little further on Rob's background. Would he make a good stepfather for Max, for example?

But then he let it all slide. He would always be there

for Max…and for Emma…if they really needed him, but he couldn't be their fallback every time the tiniest hiccup happened in their lives, and he couldn't prevent Emma from dating anyone she wanted. He said easily instead, "Right, yes, I think Jackie mentioned it. So Rob had to cancel?"

"He shouldn't have!" Emma said. "He has to start shifting his priorities now that we're getting more serious. He could have taken the first flight down tomorrow. He could have insisted that they keep the meeting to the original start time instead of pushing it forward."

"So that was why he flew down this afternoon? Because the meeting time changed?"

"He should have said he couldn't make the earlier time," Emma insisted.

"I can't imagine you doing something like this, Tucker," Mom put in helpfully.

Tucker ignored her. "But he's gone now."

"And we're supposed to have a family night without him? I'm terrible on those go-karts. Max won't have any fun at all."

"I told Emma you'd do the go-kart rides with him…" his mom said.

"Well, I—"

"…and the movie, pizza and popcorn."

Okay, no. No!

His scalp tightened. He'd been about to say that, yes, okay, he could stop in at the go-kart place and do a few laps with Max—he'd have to text Daisy and tell her he was going to be late—but the dinner plan was too much.

And in fact the go-kart plan was wrong, too, he realized. If his mom was trying to prove that he and Emma and Max made a better family than Rob and Emma and

Max did, she could just end that idea right now. It wasn't happening.

"Mom, you shouldn't have asked me to come over for something like this."

"But you're always concerned for Max's happiness."

"Max's long-term well-being, yes, but not his happiness every minute of every day. Emma, I'm sorry, I do have plans for tonight. I'm sorry Rob let you down, but he does seem to have had a reason for it. Max is ten, he's old enough to understand that plans have to change sometimes. Give him the choice. He can either do the go-karts and the movie tonight just with you, or he can wait until Rob can be a part of it, too."

Emma looked at him with those big eyes. Were the rims a little pinker? Was the new gleam in them the brimming of tears? He waited for her to up the ante and make him feel like a total heel, and suddenly he knew with startling clarity why their marriage had never turned into the real thing, as his mom still so clearly wanted. Why it had never even come close.

He'd always put it down to the lack of chemistry, but there was a lot more to it than that.

He cared about Emma and Max, and he always would, but if he'd ever cared enough to make himself emotionally vulnerable to Emma's wishes and desires, he would have made himself utterly miserable and filled with rage, and Emma and Max miserable, too.

As an aside, he realized that Daisy had never tried to manipulate him like that.

Hell, he couldn't wait to see her!

Nobody spoke. Tucker had said his piece—long, for him—and didn't have anything more to add. His mom was attempting not to interfere, now that it was clear her misguided little ploy had backfired. Emma was hoping that the brimming and blinking eyes would push him into an agreement if she just stayed quiet a little longer, although he was certain her secret agenda was much more short-term than his mother's.

"I'll head off," he announced. He looked at his watch, impatient to be out of here. The detour to his mother's had already added forty minutes to his journey from Lake Luzerne to Spruce Bay.

Emma looked shocked that he was really going, that he hadn't caved—hadn't even budged. She made a little sound and jumped to her feet, but his mom put out a warning hand.

"I guess he's right, honey," she said. "Max is old enough to wait a day or two. Rob will be back tomorrow evening." She was looking intently at Tucker and he wondered what she saw. The happiness? The all-consuming fire?

Feelings that had nothing whatsoever to do with Emma.

A part of him wanted to shout his feelings for Daisy to the rooftops, to everyone he knew. Another part of him gloried in the fact that their relationship was still so new and secret. There were some good things about easing into it, it turned out.

He hugged his mother goodbye, gave Max another swing, throwing him up to the ceiling. Emma had her arms folded as if to say, *You're not hugging me if you're going to be like this.*

He didn't care, just said a general "See you soon," and left, gunning the pickup out of his mother's driveway a little too fast for safety, and only just remembering to check in the rearview mirror that there was nothing in the way.

When he reached Spruce Bay at last, Mary Jane had apparently been waiting for him with business to attend to. She emerged from the office and he had to stop the car, when he'd planned on driving as far as the parking area adjacent to the restaurant, and his heart sank at the sight of her. He could see the lights on in there, and hoped it meant that Daisy was finishing up. They could taste test those recipes, and then…

At least Mary Jane didn't waste time getting to her point. "Can I just check with you that I've done the right thing in taking bookings for cabins three and four?" she asked.

"Didn't I say that already, yesterday?"

"But the new walkways will be done by then, will they? Definitely?"

"They will definitely be done."

"Including the pergola section?"

"Yes, absolutely. We have the footings in place already. The carpentry work will be done tomorrow. If the forecast looks iffy for next week, we'll paint over the weekend because it's supposed to be pretty mild."

"And is there any chance you can have something planted in there?"

"I can if you want. It won't be the permanent plantings. We're too close to the cold weather to get those in. But there are some temporary options."

Do we have to talk about this now?

Without waiting for her to answer, he added impatiently, "Is Daisy around? Over in the restaurant?"

"Yes, still working on the recipes. She wanted us to eat over there tonight, give her some feedback and help her with the detail—"

"Sounds great." He went to start the engine again, but Mary Jane wasn't done.

"But she was later starting on it than she wanted. We're getting a little behind in a few areas. I'm not sure about the eating plan. I know she'll get distracted as soon as she sees you, and if we don't get our recipes finalized, with ingredients and quantities noted down—"

"Get distracted?"

"I'm thinking maybe she and I should do the taste testing on our own. Could you wait a couple hours, Tucker? Come back when we're all done?"

"You want me to leave." Every cell in his body rebelled. Hadn't he waited long enough already? He hadn't seen Daisy all day, and he could picture her, feel the scent of her on his skin in anticipation, and it just seemed impossible to keep waiting. "You want me just to go and fill in time? Because I'm a distraction?"

"We have our first booking in less than a week," she reminded him, although he knew it perfectly well.

"Didn't you say Daisy wanted my help?"

Mary Jane laughed. "Help." She crooked her fingers into imaginary quotation marks. "Well, she might, but I've seen that kind of help before." Suddenly, to his eyes she looked so shrewish, standing there, her body stiffened against the cold of early evening, while he sat impatiently at the wheel. She had her arms folded and her eyes narrowed and she looked like an unhappy woman taking her bitterness out on everything around her. "I don't think we have time for it tonight, Tucker."

Which was when he lost it.

"Why do you not want this to happen?" He could see the windows of the restaurant kitchen all steamed up, could imagine Daisy darting around there in the warmth, surrounded by delectable aromas, and all he wanted—*all* he wanted, damn it, was it so much to ask?—was to be with her.

Hold her.

Bury his face in her hair.

Laugh with her.

Wash her cooking pots and make lists of grocery orders, if need be.

His whole body ached with it like an illness.

"I've just told you why I don't want it. She's behind. We both are. And if that means we have unhappy guests next week—"

"I'm not talking about you not wanting me to go over there right now," he cut in impatiently. "Although that's bad enough. I'm talking about the whole relationship. My relationship with Daisy, Mary Jane. You don't want it. Whether that's on Lee's behalf or your own, I don't know."

"She hasn't told Lee yet."

He read the words as a challenge and a dismissal.

She hasn't told Lee yet because you're not nearly as important as you think.

"And you're happy about that, aren't you?" he accused. His temples were throbbing with tension. "How do you have the interfering audacity to feel that way? How can you be such a bitch?" The words came out with no thought for politeness or censorship or kindness. His need for Daisy was as powerful as an addiction, and after Emma and his mother both attempting to waylay him, his impatience had built up a powerful head of steam. "Of all people, Mary Jane, you are the one who should understand."

Did she even remember? Daisy up in her room with the light shining out, Tucker looking up at her as if she was Juliet, Mary Jane coming out and catching him, and him catching her catching him, and them both knowing, and nothing being said...

Did she remember that?

He saw in her face that she did, that she knew exactly what he was talking about, and told her even more forcefully, "You do understand, damn it, but you want to sabotage it. You want to scuttle it."

"That's not fair!"

"It's the same as it was ten years ago. You were un-happy with Alex, it wasn't going where you wanted, so you didn't want anyone else to get there first, and espe-cially not your baby sister. You couldn't stand for her to be happy when you weren't, and ten years later you're exactly the same. Maybe worse."

"That is really, really unfair, Tucker." She looked at him as if he'd slapped her, her cheeks suddenly bright pink and her eyes glittering, and he was so far gone that he didn't even care.

Her problem, wasn't it?

He revved the engine and the pickup surged forward, leaving a spit of icy gravel in its wake. Ahead, the golden light spilled through the steamy restaurant windows and he just couldn't wait another moment.

Seeing Daisy was everything he'd wanted, everything he'd been hanging out for all day.

He leaped from the car, ran up the steps to the staff entrance, pushed open the door and there she was. She beamed at him, standing at the long workbench with her hands deep in a pair of red oven mitts, placing a pie on a rack to cool. "Hi... Want to taste?"

She meant the pie. "Wanna taste you first," he growled. He stepped forward and claimed her completely for him-self, wrapping her in his arms, smelling the sweetness of sugar and fruit that enveloped her. She had a tiny smear of something sticky and red on her cheek. He nuzzled his lips against it and tasted cranberry.

Her mouth was cranberry flavored, too, tart and sugary and delicious, and her whole body was so soft and warm. At the taste and feel of her, heat arrowed instantly to his groin and he felt himself getting hard, pressing against her. She felt it and responded, rocking her hips in a sinuous rhythm that made him crazy with wanting her. They were locked together so close, it was like they were two trees planted in the same spot, growing together.

He touched her everywhere he could reach, running his hands down her back, cupping her sweet butt, feeling her breasts squashed soft against his chest. She belonged in his arms like this and he didn't give a damn about the recipes, even though the scent of them was so good in the air.

Or about Mary Jane, even though, yeah, he'd probably upset her a bit, he knew.

Hell, she'd upset him first!

Daisy murmured, "Mmm" and he kissed her throat, feeling the vibration of the soft moans she wasn't trying to suppress. When she cooked, she always put her hair in a messy knot, and tendrils always escaped. Devouring her mouth, he felt the tickle of those fragrant strands against his cheek, and reached back to pull the hair free of its elastic band. It fell, sweeping against his face like a caress.

He wanted her so badly that he started thinking about kitchen countertops, or, better, the lounge section of the restaurant's small bar. There was a long, thickly padded leather bench seat in there, brand-new...

Daisy suddenly pulled away. "What was that car?"

"What car?"

"I heard a car roaring out of here like it was in a police chase, over by the office."

He hadn't heard a thing.

"Mary Jane's on her own over there," Daisy said. "If some lunatic is doing burnouts in our parking lot..."

She hurried out to the restaurant and over to the huge plate-glass sliding doors that overlooked the new section of deck, pulling one open and slipping out. Tucker followed her into the cold dark.

The engine noise wasn't a stranger doing burnouts.

Tucker and Daisy both arrived in time to see the sudden red of brake lights glowing against the blue of Mary Jane's car. Something had run across the driveway, a squirrel or a raccoon, and she'd braked to avoid hitting it. As soon as the route was clear she was off again, driving too fast on the resort's winding private-access road.

"Something's happened," Daisy said. "Mom and Dad, or..." She whirled away from the windows and took a few steps, then stopped. "But why didn't she come over? Has she sent me a text I missed? She doesn't usually drive like that."

Tucker said what he knew to be true. "It's my fault."

"Yours?"

"Just now when I drove in, before I came over here."

"Oh, you saw her?"

"She came out. We talked a bit. She didn't want me interrupting you while you were working on the recipes. You had a plan for taste testing over dinner, and she didn't think I should be part of it. We argued about it."

"Must have been quite an argument," she said lightly. Light on the surface, wary beneath. "To interrupt or not to interrupt. Who knew that could be so contentious."

Shoot...

"I said too much," he admitted.

"Too much of what."

Hell, he couldn't say this, couldn't give her the details.

I wanted to see you, and she was stalling me, telling me to leave, so I basically told her her whole life was a walking disaster, to make her get out of my way.

Yeah, that sounded good.

He'd behaved impeccably over the whole incident.

Not.

"This is a mess," he muttered.

And so fast, too. He'd gone in a couple minutes from

aching for Daisy so hard that all he could think about was getting her clothes off, to realizing he was a complete—

Well, there were a lot of words for it, and most of them had four letters. He said a few of them in his head, and it didn't help.

Why had he done it? Sure, Mary Jane had been pretty irritating, so certain that he would be a hindrance to Daisy's preparations, tight-mouthed and disapproving about it, but still… Why had he let his hot, driving impatience and passion and need take control of his manners, his mouth and his basic human decency?

The problem had a familiar taste and a familiar name. *Dad.*

His father had done it more times than he could count. His father had demonstrated this same tunnel-visioned ruthlessness about his own happiness for the whole four years that he was dying. His father had fallen passionately in love, and it had changed everything, and he hadn't cared who he hurt or how much. All he'd ever seen were his own needs.

And now I'm doing the same thing.

Tucker felt sick to his stomach. "I am so sorry. I hurt her, Daisy. Probably a lot. I said something…a few things."

"What things?"

He couldn't avoid telling her, he knew that now, but he made it as brief as he could. "That she had no life, so she was trying to wreck mine."

Chapter Sixteen

"You told her *what?*"

"Don't make me repeat it," he muttered. He wasn't meeting her gaze.

"Why?"

"Because you heard me the first time."

"No, not that," Daisy almost yelled. Her throat hurt. "Why did you tell her something so hurtful?"

He said bluntly, through clenched teeth, "Because I wanted to see you, and she was getting in my way. I told her she was a bitch."

Everything was perfect, and then came the first chink in the facade.

Her stomach sank. Was this the real Tucker, self-absorbed and unkind, which she could only see once the dazzle had cleared from her eyes? He already had a broken engagement to Lee, now he'd callously hurt Mary Jane.

She was so shocked. Shocked that she might have misread him so badly. Shocked at how much that hurt. Like having something incredibly precious ripped out of her arms without the slightest warning.

She couldn't believe this was happening. She'd been yearning for him all day, and now...

Blinking back tears of acute disappointment and anger, she told him, "Do you know how much Mary Jane beats herself up about her life? About the fact that she's single? And that it makes her bitter and jealous sometimes?"

He didn't answer, just stared down, scraping the calluses on his palm with his thumb.

"She hates it, hates being like that, hates that she can't help it. I told you she was lonely, Tucker. I *gave* you that information, broke her confidence... I should never have said it... But I never, *ever* thought you would use it against her so cruelly!"

"I need to apologize. I do know that, Daisy." He looked up at last, met her gaze with a fierce light in his blue eyes.

"To her or to me?"

"To her, first." He looked terrible, almost as bad as he'd looked that night a few weeks ago at the hospital, when Kyle Schramm's mother and girlfriend had been bristling at each other with such hostility and dislike.

He gave off the same sense of intense pressure, of questioning his own reactions, of being thrown back into the past in a way that bruised him all over. A part of her ached for him. She couldn't help it. But she made herself harden her own heart.

"Then to you," he was saying. "Or to you now. But fast. Because I need to go find her."

"Don't waste time on any apology to me."

"No?"

"But don't come back after you've talked to my sister. Or call. Or expect to have me in your bed again."

Now the shock that vibrated in her body showed just as much in him. She expected an argument, expected him to pull her into his arms and try to convince her that everything was fine.

Michael would have done that. Michael would have told her she was being petty and irrational and making a mountain out of a molehill.

But Tucker didn't say a word in his own defense, nor a word to get her back in his arms. He just gave a tiny nod, as if he didn't care enough to fight her on what she'd said.

She'd just dumped him, and he wasn't even going to argue. This was the biggest shock of all.

They were still standing on the deck in the cold, and he didn't go back through the kitchen, just thumped down the steps and around the side of the restaurant to his car, keys already in hand. "I will fix this with Mary Jane," he said, blue eyes still blazing. "Even if I can't...don't have the right...to fix it with you."

He slid into the car, started the engine and drove away, chasing after her at a speed that made Mary Jane's wild flight look sedate by comparison. In moments, his taillights had disappeared.

Taillights... Fully dark already... What time was it?

Oh, Lord, the butternut and goat cheese gratin!

Daisy raced back into the kitchen and grabbed the dish from the oven just in time. It was burned around the edges but the center was fine.

If she cared.

Which she didn't.

She turned off the oven and surveyed the array of dishes she'd prepared with such excitement and such meticulous attention this afternoon.

As well as the cranberry pie and butternut gratin, there was a golden, crisp-skinned turkey with a wild mushroom and Parma ham stuffing, a pumpkin pie with nut-and-ginger topping, a dish of green beans, fennel and leeks, an earthenware pot of creamy cauliflower-and-potato soup and a baking dish filled with a very French potato dauphinoise.

Yes, she was a dessert specialist, but she was pretty good in other areas, as well. It was going to be a great meal. There was still a salad she hadn't made, and a yam dish with herb-streusel topping, which she wasn't going to get to tonight.

She'd thought that she and Tucker and Mary Jane would sit down and sample them right here in the restaurant, served just as they would be on Thanksgiving night. She'd noted down every detail on ingredient quantities and cooking time, and still had opinions to consider, and more notes to make. They needed to order some smaller casserole dishes, for example.

None of it seemed to matter right now.

Should she call Mary Jane to warn her that Tucker was coming?

She picked up her phone and stood there looking at the thumbnail picture of her sister. All she had to do was touch that section of the screen. But Mary Jane never answered her phone when she was at the wheel, and hadn't looked as if she was in any mood to pull over at the sound of her ringtone. She might drive for miles. Hours.

And what would I say? she asked herself. This whole thing was between Mary Jane and Tucker, and she could easily make it way worse for her sister if she got in the way. They were both miserable right now, but at least if Tucker could manage a decent apology, Mary Jane might not feel quite so thoroughly destroyed.

The cleanup beckoned.

It was all she could think of to do. She was all alone

here, her hands needed something practical and the kitchen was a mess. She tackled it one step at a time, loading some items into the industrial dishwasher and washing others by hand, putting away half-used ingredients, wiping down countertops.

While the food cooled.

Mary Jane came back eventually.

No Tucker.

When she heard a car, Daisy ran to the restaurant windows to check. Her heart did its sinking thing again and she cursed her own illogical emotions. She'd just broken up with him. Would she take him back so easily, if he begged?

He wasn't going to beg.

This was Mary Jane's zippy blue thing swinging into the space behind the restaurant, not Tucker's huge pickup. She parked where Tucker had—How long ago had that been? An hour?—and jumped out. Daisy was waiting for her, with questions. "Are you okay? Did you see…? Did Tucker find you? He went after you."

"He found me," Mary Jane answered shortly.

"Where?"

"Pulled over. Opposite the trail-ride place. I shouldn't have driven off like that. I skidded on a patch of frost and nearly ran off the road. Came to my senses and stopped."

"So? What did he do?"

"He apologized."

"Good."

Mary Jane nodded. "Yes. He said he'd told you." She pressed her lips together. She wasn't intending to give the details on what he'd said, either when they'd argued or when he'd apologized for it. "He said you've…ended things."

"Yes."

"You didn't have to do that. Not for my sake."

"What, I'm going to stay with a man who calls my sister a bitch?"

"He apologized."

"That's not good enough." She tried for some flippancy and achieved a very wobbly version. "Lucky I never told Lee that we were dating, hey?"

Mary Jane shot her a swift glance. "That's not really what you're thinking about."

"No."

"You're in love with him."

"I thought I was."

"You're not in love with him?"

"I'm furious with him. It's—it's the way I fell out of love with Michael. It was perfect, and then there was one chink, and the chink grew, and the whole thing cracked wide-open, and the process of dealing with that was... pretty horrible...and I'm not going through it again. I should have taken more notice of that first chink. So I am taking notice this time. I shortcut the whole process. Ended it clean."

But it didn't feel clean.

Mary Jane started making sympathetic noises. "Are you sure, Daisy?"

"What, you've been so keen for me to tell Lee in case it's a problem for her, and now there's no need, and it won't be a problem for her, and you're wanting me to rethink?"

"You've seemed so happy."

"Thought I was."

"It's...been great to see. Made me jealous sometimes, yes, which I hate—I *hate*!—but other times...really happy for you." She thought for a moment, then added, "He's—he's a decent guy, Daisy. Shoot, this is so hard for me to say, and it shouldn't be! He's a really decent guy, he's been in love with you for ten years, and the two of you should be happy together, and sure there was a chink tonight… I'm sure he's not perfect. What human being is? But the chink was partly my fault. Lots my fault. I think I was being a bitch. And I don't want to think that one argument between him and me was enough to ruin the whole thing for both of you."

"Wait a second, back up!"

"Back up where?"

"In love with me for ten *years?* No! Just…no!"

Mary Jane shrugged. "Yes. At first sight pretty much. You probably don't even remember."

"I think I would if it were true."

"You don't remember what happened? Don't remember that night?"

"Which night? The night I got back from Paris? What happened? Nothing happened."

"He and Lee went out together after dinner. When they got home, she went up to her room and shut the door. I think things were pretty rocky between them. You were in your room, and you'd left your hairbrush in my car, and you leaned out the upstairs window to call for me to bring it up. Or throw it up, actually."

"Yes, I do remember that."

"You thought it was me down below, but it was Tucker. I was on the steps. And I saw his face as he looked up at you, and I understood. He was marrying the wrong sister, and he knew it. They called off the wedding the next day."

Daisy's head was in more of a whirl than ever. "B-but nothing ever happened. Nothing! Not a look or a touch or—"

"It would have, if you hadn't left for California so soon, I'm sure of it."

"He never said a word."

"How could he say something, Daisy?"

"*You* never said a word."

"Oh, sure, I was going to create a situation where you and Lee never spoke to each other again. Life took you in other directions."

"And then life brought us back together, and you didn't want the Cherry sisters working with Reid Landscaping."

"I thought somebody might get hurt."

"And you were right."

"No, I—I was just scared."

"Scared?"

"Scared of how badly I would handle it if love's young dream happened all over again." The bitterness was back in her voice. "Instantly, like it did before. All Romeo and Juliet, effortless and beautiful, with a happy ending this time, while I was—" She broke off, and made an impatient sound. "And I hate myself." She laughed harshly, and blinked back more tears.

"No, you don't." Daisy touched her arm.

"The times I haven't felt that way have been so good. I've kept trying to hold on to those." Mary Jane didn't throw off the contact. In fact, they hugged, and it was good. "Now, just when I feel I might be winning this whole battle, you tell me there's no Tucker and Daisy for me to be happy about?"

"No, there isn't. I'm sorry."

"So am I." They hugged some more. Mary Jane was the one to get practical first. "We should taste all this, and make sure it's all doable for a big crowd, too." She swept a hand over the countertop, where Daisy's dishes sat waiting.

"My heart's not in it." *My heart has gone.*

"No, mine isn't, either. But let's do it anyhow."

Chapter Seventeen

Fork, fork, knife, knife, spoon. Fork, fork, knife, knife, spoon...

The restaurant tables were covered in snowy cloths and Daisy was laying out silverware beside the gleaming white china plates. In the kitchen, new and returning staff had begun preparing tomorrow's lavish Thanksgiving meal. They were fully booked, with local people, resort guests and tourists staying elsewhere.

Whether it was the time of day they'd chosen that had made the event so popular, or the menu, or the lure of an opening celebration, Daisy didn't know. Or maybe it was none of those things. There seemed to be a lot of local goodwill toward Spruce Bay Resort. She'd taken several phone calls for bookings, in which the caller expressed their best wishes for her mom and dad's retirement, and fondness for Mary Jane. People were rooting for the resort's renovation to succeed.

And I want that, too. I just wish I could feel right now.

All she could really think about was Tucker. Missing him. Wanting him. Questioning her own behavior. For the past week, she had seen him almost every day, and yet she felt as if she hadn't seen him at all. They'd both been ferociously busy with preparations for the reopening and the festive meal, with Daisy working indoors and Tucker seemingly everywhere at once.

At least three times she'd looked out the restaurant windows at the sound of an engine, hoping it was one of the Reid Landscaping pickups, with Tucker's familiar silhouette at the wheel. Yesterday, she'd gone over to the cabins to place the fresh towels and soaps in the brand-new bathrooms and had heard his voice coming from down near the lake, where the steps and walkways were almost completed.

"Left, Kyle. No, it's not level. Back it up a bit."

New kitchen hand Molly appeared at that moment with a tray of wineglasses, and it happened again—the Reid Landscaping truck went by, heading toward the lake, with Tucker driving. "Are they going to be finished in time?" Molly asked. "There's still nothing in the planter boxes on the deck."

"They'll be finished," Daisy said. Yesterday, Tucker hadn't left until after dark. Today, she knew he'd be here till midnight if he had to, and again at the crack of dawn tomorrow.

"They seem like a great crew," Molly chattered happily, sounding like the teenager she was. "Tucker is pretty cool, a really nice guy. I was talking to him yesterday when he was dumping soil into the planters. Seems very hands-on."

"He is. He is a nice guy."

And he was so different from Michael. Michael wouldn't have behaved the way Tucker had this past week.

Michael would have been in her face, making her know down to the last detail how much this was totally her fault. Tucker was so different.

Yes, he'd made a mistake last week, brushing aside Mary Jane so hurtfully, but at least he'd apologized for it. Daisy was beginning to think that her own mistake had been much bigger. She'd let her bad experience with one man cloud her judgment of another.

Tucker wasn't Michael.

She wanted so badly to give him another chance. To give *herself* another chance. The most painful thing of all was that he didn't seem to want one.

"He is a nice guy," she repeated to Molly. "Funny and smart and hardworking. Always tries to do the right thing for the people he cares about. And when he makes a mistake, he admits it."

I need to admit it, too. And I need to give us both a better shot at this. It's too good to let go. I'm not going to accept him pushing me away without a fight. It hurts too much.

The pickup came back the other way.

"Molly, can you finish here? I need a word with Tucker." She dropped her tray of silverware on the table and went for the deck door and down the steps. The pickup was already halfway to the place where the driveway disappeared into the trees. She ran, saw the truck gain speed, almost gave up.

But finally Tucker had seen her in his mirror. He stopped and she caught up, breathless. He slid his window down and put his elbow on the sill, his mouth steady and his expression shuttered. "Sorry, I didn't see you. I'm picking up the plants for the planter boxes. Is there a problem?"

"Can we talk?"

"Yes, we can talk. If you want."

"Not like this."

"Like how, then?"

"Don't." The intimacy between them was still there. She could feel it like a force, or a hot thickness in the air. It cut through everything, despite how much he was clearly trying to shut it out. It let them talk in short snatches and still say a huge amount, it made both of them dizzy and lost, and she wasn't going to let him ignore it.

"Come sit in the truck, then," he said, voice slurred with reluctance. "I'll pull over all the way."

She climbed in and he drove another twenty yards to where there was room on the shoulder of the driveway. He switched off the engine, leaned on the wheel and looked at her with suffering in his blue eyes, and they sat in the quiet, confined space of the truck cab, and she didn't know where to begin.

In the end she just cut to the heart of it. "You made one mistake, and I was wrong to react so strongly. You apologized to Mary Jane, and now it's my turn to apologize to you. I'm sorry, Tucker. I know you wouldn't shoot your mouth off like that and just let it go. You were…tired, or something. You weren't thinking straight."

She touched his arm. It had been a starting point for them before, but today he didn't return her touch or lean closer, and all she could feel was muscle rock hard with tension beneath her fingers.

"Stop making excuses for me," he muttered.

"I'm not. I'm saying I understand." But she took her hand away, since he so clearly didn't want it there.

"You don't. You can't." The expression on his face was as solid as a brick wall.

"Then tell me," she said softly.

"I have told you. I've told you a lot of it. About my father."

"How is this…us…anything to do with your father?"

"He hurt so many people with his self-absorption, with the unlimited license he gave himself to follow his needs and emotions wherever they led. I caught myself behaving the same way and I didn't like it and I'm not going to let it happen again."

"You apologized to Mary Jane."

"And how many times can I keep doing that? Who else am I going to hurt? How long does the list have to get, Daisy, before it includes you, with your name in really big letters at the very top? How will you feel then? Will you keep letting me off the hook, the way you're trying to do now?"

"You're making too much of this. You're making yourself into a monster that doesn't exist."

"I'm not." He clenched his teeth around the words.

"How do you know that?"

"Because I lived with it for four years. I saw it in action. I saw how ruthlessly selfish someone can get when their heart dictates their actions. Feelings are an incredibly unreliable compass to point our direction."

"They can be. They're not always. Not when they match everything else. Head and logic and faith."

"Human beings need something else. We need right and wrong. We need rules and—I don't know what the word is. Precepts, or something. The sanctity of marriage. Do unto others. We *need* that stuff!"

He thumped his hand on the wheel so hard it must have hurt, but that was nothing compared to the hurt inside him, and suddenly she could see it.

See all of it.

See down to the why of it, and the stubbornness of it, and exactly where it had come from.

But still she kept trying to argue the unarguable. "And you have it, don't you?" she said.

"Yes, I have it, and that means you have to get out of the car and let this go." He was practically trembling, she could see, with his effort at staying in control, at winning over those feelings he distrusted so much. He was beating himself up as much as he was shattering her. "I'll drive you back if you like," he offered, so wooden and polite she would have laughed in any other situation but this.

Would have laughed if she hadn't been so painfully close to tears.

"No, thanks. I'll walk." She opened the door, and didn't even try to touch him because she knew he wouldn't accept it. He was good at pushing her away when he really tried.

"Seriously, I can drive you."

"Seriously, Tucker, I'm going to walk because I need to breathe some air." Her cheeks felt flushed, and beyond the hurt at their failure to get past this, she was *angry* suddenly, but it was a very different kind of anger to what she'd felt last week after Tucker's exchange with Mary Jane.

She understood a whole lot more now, and she was helplessly, passionately angry with Tucker's dad.

Done.

Tucker smoothed the soil around the last of the plants in the final planter box on the restaurant deck and stood to stretch his back. He was really done. Every walkway swept clear of dirt, every winking white fairy light strung around pergola frames and deck railings. Every piece of mess from the work cleaned up, and every tool loaded into the back of the pickup.

The rest of the Reid Landscaping crew had the day off for Thanksgiving, but Tucker hadn't planned to stop until the work was truly done. He'd started at seven this morning, before the sun was even up, and there'd already been lights on in the restaurant kitchen.

Daisy, probably.

It was after eleven in the morning now, and more people had arrived to work. He could hear voices in there, and the clang of pots and pans. He could smell the cooking, too—the most delectable aromas of onions and bacon and roasting turkey.

He had to go tell someone that his own work was complete, and he could feel his heart beating faster as he thought about it. He would go knock at the staff entrance to the kitchen, and maybe it would be Daisy who opened it, and he wanted it to be Daisy, and he really, really didn't *want* to want it that much.

Suck it up, Tucker, just get it done and go.

He was due at his mother's at noon.

He knocked, and yes.

Her.

Wearing her white cook's jacket and those blue-and-white-checked pants, looking trim and busy and a little messy, with a smear of flour on her cheek and tiny wisps of hair escaping from a net.

"Finished," he said, clearing his throat. "I'm heading off. Jackie will email the final invoice, and if there are any problems we'll be back to fix them as soon as you let us know."

She nodded. "Okay, thanks."

And he couldn't move.

She seemed to be having the same trouble. They stood

there looking at each other, and it was beyond horrible, and he didn't know what to say.

"Tell me you don't want me, Tucker," she blurted out. "Can you do that? Can you tell me we're not both standing here, burning for each other, connected down to our bones?"

Yeah, but it wasn't relevant, it wasn't what counted.

"Ten years ago," he told her, "if you'd given the slightest sign that you were feeling the same as I was, I would have thrown your sister over without a second's pause for thought. I did throw her over. We're all just lucky that she and your parents never made the connection. We're lucky Mary Jane kept her mouth shut."

She was furious. Her glare almost hit him in the face, with a blazing energy that he would have flinched from if he hadn't been holding himself so tight.

"I'm sorry you're angry—" he began.

But she wouldn't let him finish. "You might be sorry I'm angry, but you have no idea why. Do you know what your problem is, Tucker? Do you know what's really happening here? I'll tell you. I wasn't going to. I've been stewing over it, feeling so powerless. How can you fight an enemy who doesn't exist anymore?"

"Doesn't exist?"

"Maybe you're not ready to hear this, and maybe you never will be, but here it is anyhow. You won't stop beating yourself up because you never got to beat up your dad."

"What?"

"You're beating yourself up, you've been beating yourself up on and off your entire adult life when it comes to sex and love because you never got the chance to beat up your father." Her voice gentled a little. "And you never can get that chance, so shouldn't you let it go? Find a way to move on? I've had to learn that you're not the man who gave me grief in California. You need to learn that you're not your dad, and that beating yourself up isn't ever, *ever* going to settle the score with him."

The words hit him so hard, he couldn't speak.

Beat up his dad.

Beat up his *father*.

Hell, yes!

He pictured it. Eighteen-year-old self yelling, punching walls, cracking a blow across his father's face, knocking him to the floor.

Knocking him from his hospital bed.

Of course he'd never done it. He'd thought about it, and had been racked with guilt every time.

How did Daisy *know*? She was standing there, waiting for a reaction, her body soft with empathy and understanding, and shaky—he could see it—with all the things that were trembling inside him.

He still couldn't speak. Not about this anyhow. It was too new. Too shocking.

Too true?

In a splintered voice he repeated, "Jackie will send the invoice," and got himself out of there. Down the steps. Over to the pickup. Numb hand pushing in the key.

Daisy was watching him. He knew she was, even though he hadn't turned to check. He just knew she'd be standing there, hanging on the doorknob, watching him leave, not understanding what she'd done to him.

Because he still didn't understand, himself.

Made everything better?

Made everything worse…

He stopped in at the apartment for a shower, the office and showroom and yard of the business he was so proud of silent and unattended below, and arrived at his mom's on time. Mattie and Carla were there; Carla with Adam and the kids, Mattie with a new girlfriend who seemed to be fitting in just fine.

Who can I talk to about this?

It was the wrong time, the wrong occasion. And yet when they sat down to the big midday meal and he looked around him at his family, what Daisy had said made total sense. He wanted to beat up his father and he couldn't, so he was beating himself up instead, demanding an impossible standard of perfection in his own behavior as a bizarre kind of punishment delivered to the man who'd loomed so large in his adolescent life.

See, Dad? You couldn't do it, but I can. This is how to behave, Dad. I'll show you...

The feeling of light shed over his inner workings was suddenly euphoric.

This.

This is why some things have seemed so hard. This is what I've been doing to myself, and I don't have to, I can just stop.

And Daisy was the one who knew.

Of course she was the one who knew.

It was a really nice meal, a great meal, long and lazy and with way too much food. Carla and Mattie had grown into such great people. Adam, Carla's husband, adored his wife and kids. The new girlfriend, Alice, laughed at everything Mattie said, and gave as good as she got. They worked as a couple, and he got the feeling she might be around for a while. He stayed until after five, helping to clean up but resisting his mom's and Mattie's pleas for him to sit and watch football.

And then he just couldn't wait any longer.

"Mom, I'm going. There's something I need to do."

* * *

It was dark when he reached Spruce Bay. The restaurant was all lit up, inside and out, and the extended deck looked just the way he'd envisaged, inviting and beautiful. Their meal had been scheduled for a four o'clock start, so it was still going. As he climbed out of the pickup, he could hear laughter and conversation and music.

Was it crazy to be here?

Yes, since he still didn't know exactly what he was going to do. Thank her?

Apologize...*again?*

He went to the wide steps that led up to the deck and just stood there, looking inside. He saw Daisy bringing out desserts. They were serving them family style, setting down whole pies on the tables and cutting slices right there, adding ice cream or whipped cream. She looked busy and flushed and she was smiling.

He didn't need to hear what everyone was saying to know that the meal had been a huge success. She was right in the middle of it, taking the praise, passing out pie, hips sliding between the crowded, happy tables, wearing the chef's uniform that made her look so neat and competent and...well...beautiful. Always. He couldn't take his eyes off her, but she didn't see him at all.

Mary Jane did.

She froze for a moment, then gestured at him, making a round-the-back movement with her finger, before disappearing into the kitchen and emerging through the staff door in time to meet his hurried approach.

What did he look like? He had no idea, but she must have seen something. "You're here for Daisy." A statement, not a question.

He said, suffering, "Mary Jane, I need...I need your permission. Don't I?"

There was a beat of silence, then she said with conviction, "No, you don't. You need Lee's."

"Lee's?"

"Yes. If you need anyone's permission, it's Lee's. Not that I'm telling you you have to get it, but you look like you need *something,* some way to move forward."

"I do."

"So call Lee. Come on, I'll take you over to the office where it's quiet. I'm sensing you're not in a patient mood right now, so just do it."

He did it.

Got her on the second ring.

"Hey, Lee? It's Tucker…"

Mary Jane stood in the doorway with her arms folded and listened to the whole conversation, the way his mother used to stand over him sometimes when he was a kid tidying his room. When it was done, with a lot of confession on his side and some very generous and sensible words on Lee's, Mary Jane was smiling. "See why I never wanted to see her hurt?"

"She's a great woman. I never doubted that."

"Just not the right woman."

"Just not. Daisy is. She told me something today… She saw something in me…" He shook his head. Couldn't say it. Not to anyone but Daisy herself. Hell, he was going to cry if he didn't get this done! "Is she still frantic in there?" He tilted his head in the direction of the restaurant.

"She's good. If she's still cutting pie, I'll take over."

"Thanks. You're the best."

"Go. I'll close up in here." She shooed him out of the office as if he was a stray puppy, and he sprinted back across the grounds because he might die if he didn't get this said…done…in the next two minutes.

When Daisy saw him appear in the kitchen—she was

standing by the sink, unloading a vast pile of plates—her eyes went wide and her mouth went soft and that gave him hope. "I'm sorry," he said.

"For what?" She wiped her hands on her jacket and stepped away from the sink toward him. She touched her hair and he wanted to pull off the net and bury his face in those golden strands, but not yet, not yet, they had to talk first.

"You know for what. For taking so long to understand myself. For letting it hurt you, even for a minute. What you said…about not beating up my dad. All sorts of things have been about doing that. Trying to do it. Trying to punish him when he was beyond punishment. Getting engaged to Lee when we should only ever have been friends. Marrying Emma to help her and Max, and then feeling bad for Mom and Max, and even for Jackie, for heck's sake, that my marriage never turned into the real thing, even though Emma never wanted it to."

"Oh, Tucker…" She reached him and looked up into his face, and did what she'd done so many times before. She touched his arm. Asking him. And the answer was yes.

Yes, Daisy. I want you. I love you.

"And then you said it," he told her. "And it was like a shaft of sun hitting a rock. It freed me. It just did. Made something click in my head. Like the lock turning on a prison door. I thought about it. Had Thanksgiving with my family, with it going round and round in my mind and making more and more sense. And then I came back here, because…hell…you don't know how impatient I got after that. And I called Lee."

"Lee?"

"I needed to. Mary Jane helped with that."

"And Lee—"

"—is great. The best. But she's not you."

"So…"

"Apparently I didn't need her permission, but I got it anyhow, and I'm here."

"You can tell I'm happy about that…" She was smiling, reaching up to his face.

"I want you in my life, Daisy. For always. I want to marry you. If it's not too soon for me to say that."

"Oh, it's not!"

"Is it ten years too late?"

"It's not that, either… You know."

"So say it for me right now. Say we'll get married." He dipped closer, brushed his mouth across hers, light yet lingering. "Because I'm going crazy over this."

She chased the contact and pressed her parted lips against his. He felt the dart of her tongue and the delectable, plummy softness of her mouth. She tasted of ice cream, and she whispered against his skin, "Please, can we get married, Tucker? And can we do it soon?"

He kissed her again, sweet and deep, while the Thanksgiving party went on beyond the closed kitchen door. "I want you for my wife so much, Daisy Cherry."

"I want you, too," she whispered. "For everything. Forever."

And as he held her, he just knew, down to his bones, what he'd known in his heart for so long—that this was right.

* * * * *

A sneaky peek at next month...

Cherish™

ROMANCE TO MELT THE HEART EVERY TIME

My wish list for next month's titles...

In stores from 20th September 2013:

☐ The Christmas Baby Surprise – Shirley Jump

& A Weaver Beginning – Allison Leigh

☐ Single Dad's Christmas Miracle – Susan Meier

& Snowbound with the Soldier – Jennifer Faye

In stores from 4th October 2013:

☐ A Maverick for Christmas – Leanne Banks

& Her Montana Christmas Groom – Teresa Southwick

☐ The Redemption of Rico D'Angelo – Michelle Douglas

& The Rancher's Christmas Princess – Christine Rimmer

Available at WHSmith, Tesco, Asda, Eason, Amazon and Apple

Just can't wait?

Wrap up warm this winter with Sarah Morgan...

Sleigh Bells in the Snow

Kayla Green loves business and hates Christmas.

So when Jackson O'Neil invites her to Snow Crystal Resort to discuss their business proposal… the last thing she's expecting is to stay for Christmas dinner. As the snowflakes continue to fall, will the woman who doesn't believe in the magic of Christmas finally fall under its spell…?

4th October

www.millsandboon.co.uk/sarahmorgan

1013/MB435

She's loved and lost — will she ever
learn to open her heart again?

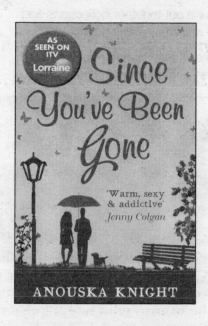

From the winner of ITV Lorraine's Racy Reads,
Anouska Knight, comes a heart-warming tale of
love, loss and confectionery.

'The perfect summer read — warm,
sexy and addictive!'
—Jenny Colgan

For exclusive content visit:
www.millsandboon.co.uk/anouskaknight

 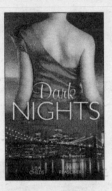 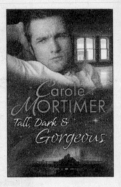

Join the Mills & Boon Book Club

Subscribe to **Cherish**™ today for 3, 6 or 12 months and you could **save over £40!**

We'll also treat you to these fabulous extras:

- 🌹 **FREE L'Occitane gift set worth £10**
- 🌹 **FREE home delivery**
- 🌹 **Rewards scheme, exclusive offers…and much more!**

Subscribe now and save over £40
www.millsandboon.co.uk/subscribeme

The World of Mills & Boon®

There's a Mills & Boon® series that's perfect for you. We publish ten series and, with new titles every month, you never have to wait long for your favourite to come along.

Blaze.
Scorching hot, sexy reads
4 new stories every month

By Request
Relive the romance with the best of the best
9 new stories every month

Cherish™
Romance to melt the heart every time
12 new stories every month

Desire™
Passionate and dramatic love stories
8 new stories every month